IS THAT YOU,
JOHN WAYNE?

IS THAT YOU, JOHN WAYNE?

short (and shorter) stories

SCOTT GARSON

Queen's Ferry Press

Queen's Ferry Press
8240 Preston Road
Suite 125-151
Plano, TX 75024
www.queensferrypress.com

Published 2013 by Queen's Ferry Press

Cover design by Jason Hieronymus

First edition April 2013

ISBN 978-1-938466-07-6

Printed in the United States of America

PRAISE FOR IS THAT YOU, JOHN WAYNE?

"The way I feel about this book is the way one of Scott Garson's original, unsparing characters feels about the moon: 'She thought it was beautiful but thought this was beside the point. She thought it was real. It was wild and actual. It was pulling her out to sea.' These wild, actual stories, whether spun over years and pages or distilled into a few words, conjure humor, loss, and moments of startling wisdom. They are beautiful, but also real, and Garson's command of the strangeness in even everyday moments pulls us outside of our everyday lives."

—Caitlin Horrocks, author of *This Is Not Your City*

"This was exactly the book I needed to read right now. I'm not sure how Scott Garson manages the precision of his narratives, the way he uncovers the exact moment, however inconsequential it may seem at first, when the world takes on a new shape for his characters. That he can temper this with a strange, sneaky humor makes *Is That You, John Wayne?* a very special collection."

—Kevin Wilson, author of *The Family Fang*

PRAISE FOR AMERICAN GYMNOPÉDIES

"Like Erik Satie's *Gymnopédies*, Garson's atmospheric shorts surprised me with their subtle shifts and eccentricities. Linked by geographic places, the collection progresses in tiny increments to become a dance between internal and external geographies. In perception and execution, this is a wonderfully original work."
   —Jim Heynen, author of *The One-Room Schoolhouse*

"Scott Garson concocts, in *American Gymnopédies*, a diabolical geography of loss out of an atlas of jim-dandy and crackerjack, snapshotting the American township grid, netting up the world in a strung-out string theory of gorgeous adhesive prose . . . This map is more detailed than the things it represents. What distortion! What projection! What treasure!"
   —Michael Martone, author of *Four for a Quarter*

for Becky

CONTENTS

STARTS

My niece was playing crazy eights with her friend from the other side of the cornfield. On her father's—my brother's—futon couch, I was trying to start reading a novel. This novel had my brother's fervent approval. He'd taken it down from his shelves. He'd gripped its lower corners in both hands and straightened its edge toward me in ceremonial transfer. So I wanted to like it. I wouldn't have minded being lifted or mentally changed. But I kept slipping out.

Clovers, my niece told her friend.

I said, Clubs.

I call them clovers, she said.

I said, I call pudding 'firewood.'

I was ignored.

You want some firewood for dessert? I've got some really good chocolate firewood.

I couldn't get back to my reading; I kept hearing the words I'd just said.

And then I was thinking: about how, a few days before, I'd messed up and taken a left on a road that had entered the green of cemetery. I didn't know this cemetery. I stopped and got out of the car. For a while I looked at the gravestones in the grass of the valley below.

I looked at the open sky to the east, and the clouds, which dragged their shadows toward a farm and a line of big windmills.

In the book I was reading, or trying to read, that moment would have been lodged, I guessed, in backstory, the weight of the past. There would have been some kind of meaning in what the man felt as he stood by the door of his car with those trampled receipts on the floor mat. The tale might have been about him and his brother, or him and their grandpa, who'd died. It would have been about something. Guy visits his brother. It's August. It's hot. Something is happening. Something or other begins to take shape within the loose blow of his days.

THE FAKE I.D.

She didn't believe that anyone could believe that she was this person. This person had a weighty face. It looked weighty. Full of bone. The name was 'Danna'—Danna Hollenfar.

Danna was, by printed date, twenty-two years old. In the photo, her mouth and nose were pulled to one side, like she was resisting a joke. But her eyes looked frank and hard.

"Danna Hollenfar," she said out loud. She was doing her eyes in the mirror. "1311 Rand Boulevard."

The boy at the door of the club, however, was too coked up to ask questions.

The warm-up band, X-25, was not a band but a person. He had a long, creased face. He sat on a wooden stool and messed with an electric guitar.

Because her friend, Janette, was drunk, and because she wasn't friends with anyone else in the surrounding darkness, she listened to the songs that X-25 sang. In the light of the stage, which was hard and square, he looked tall and bent and tired. He seemed quiet by nature. Between songs he said things, though.

She had the idea that he had the idea that no one

there was listening. In fact, no one was. In the giant black-walled space, voices rolled and boomed.

Janette—her friend—got sick in the alley just as the second band came on. She pulled Janette's blonde hair from her face and secured it with her own black tie.

"She's fine," said a person named Rolley after Janette rose and left for the restroom.

She nodded.

She knew the line from the chorus of the song the second band was playing now—"Gonna hop a star." But through the walls of the building the song was muffled. "Danna Hollenfar," she heard. "Danna Hollenfar."

Rolley had a backstage pass and got her in to look for Janette because Janette could not be found.

"*Who* are you looking for?" X-25 asked.

"Her name is Janette," she said to him. "She lives at 26 Old Peach Road with her parents, who are happily married. She plays violin. She was on the swim team until two weeks ago. She didn't like it. She quit."

X-25 sat blinking at her.

She gleamed with the odd magnificence of her lie, of how she'd told it. All of these things were true, in fact; all of them were true about her.

They didn't stay for the headliners. They walked to a sliver of park and claimed a slat bench across from another bench where a shirtless man lay sleeping.

X-25 rolled cigarettes and pressed hashish in the tips.

"People weren't listening to you," she said, and

watched the roll of smoke she breathed as it pulled toward the flickering streetlight.

"Big black box full of assholes," he said. "I told them. *You all look like assholes.*"

"You didn't say that."

"*Are you assholes? You're assholes, huh?*"

"You didn't say that," she said. "I'd have heard."

He nodded in a slow and private way, as if he was harboring menace.

"What's your name?" she asked.

"What's yours?" he countered.

She nodded, a little like he had.

Then they were in this overgrown field surrounded by huge apartment blocks. In fact, it had been a baseball field. A chain-link backstop, ten feet high, was chiming in sudden wind.

She watched the moon, which was crisp and round and pulling from layers of fleet, gauzy cloud. She said, "Moon." She thought it was beautiful but thought this was beside the point. She thought it was real. It was wild and actual. It was pulling her out to sea.

X-25 had the right idea. He'd stretched himself out like an *X* on the rise where the pitcher's mound had been.

"Probably your friend took a cab," he said.

"Do you think I'm thinking about that?"

He didn't answer.

"I'm sure she did," she continued. "I'm sure she's asleep in her bed."

She could almost see it.

He took a slow breath.

"Can I call you X?" she asked.

"You can call me whatever you want."

She knelt and then lay down beside him and put her right hand on his chest.

"Say something," she told him.

"What," he responded.

"I want to feel your voice."

"I like you. You're somebody in this world who I like."

"That could be a song."

"Uh-huh."

She lifted her hand to shutter the light of the moon. "I could feel it," she said.

DEMONS

Last winter I lived above a postal services shop which shall remain unnamed. The place was well-heated. This, for me, was its primary virtue. It was so warm that I could open the front windows and get the hard air and the sudden intimate sound of tires as they moved through gray slush.

There was another place in the back. I may never have met its sole tenant, Clark Minds, if I hadn't had to find work and chosen to try the shop downstairs for reasons that will be obvious if you've lived through an Iowa winter.

My entrance rang bells.

But I wasn't acknowledged by either the manager, a guy named Thompson Leach, whom I'd met at a party a while before, or by the patron, Clark Minds, whom I wouldn't know personally for another few days. By birth I'm a Pisces, and am often ignored.

Clark Minds and Thompson Leach were speaking across the counter about the former man's post-office box.

Clark Minds said, "The item I'm expecting . . ." and then said it again.

Thompson Leach stared across the counter at Clark

Minds with what I would have to call hatred.

"The item I'm expecting . . . It's very important."

"Try tomorrow," said Thompson Leach.

"Yes." Two things you have to know about Clark Minds: he grimaces when he talks, and he says 'yes' in a singular way, with a huge effort of concentration. I've sometimes wondered what would happen to him if he ever failed in this effort.

"It's been put in a neighboring box, could be," said Clark Minds.

"You said that."

"Yes," said Clark Minds.

"You said that about the neighboring box. Do you remember?"

Clark Minds turned from the counter for a moment. Sensing my presence, he swung toward me a broad face that swam with alarm. Flesh rolled his stubbled nape.

"This is an extremely difficult situation," he told Thompson Leach at a discreet volume.

"There's nothing difficult about it."

"I don't mean to imply wrongdoing. I'd be the first to agree with you that mistakes are just part of the plan."

"Are they just part of the plan?" blurted Thompson Leach.

The other man grimaced.

"Try tomorrow."

"Yes," Clark Minds said.

"Tomorrow."

Clark Minds turned. He was a short guy, about ten years older than me. As he made his way to the bell-hung door, he flicked me a bogus smile.

At whose party had I made the acquaintance of Thompson Leach? In what neighborhood? How long before?

I remember just this: as we two were being introduced, he'd looked away. It was as if this exchange of our names was a painful humiliation for him.

Also this: as I'd crossed a string-lit room where Thompson Leach played his guitar, he hadn't looked at me, or at the other few people in the room, his small audience. He'd kept his chin tucked away. We'd seen only his ponytail.

I think he was thinking he recognized me too when I told him I was looking for work. I think I probably benefited from his associating me with a different part of his life.

I started the next Monday. I won't bore you with the particulars of the job. They bored me enough while I had it. They bored Thompson Leach too. I was pretty happy to see that. I was happy to know I'd be working for someone who wouldn't judge me for not taking a keen interest.

Thompson Leach seemed apologetic almost each time he had to give me instruction. He seemed to be saying, You've surely got better things to consider . . .

I was like, No, no.

The other employees were younger. Claude and Nina. They were both still in school. Thompson Leach didn't look their way very often. When addressing them, he spoke under his breath.

For a place without noticeable power tensions, the

shop was unusually drear.

It was maybe best toward closing. Out the windows the day would turn blue. Motes of dry, colorless snow would appear. Spooled woolen scarves and tapering hoods would smoke with people's breath.

It was also good in the morning when certain of the people who had post-office boxes would unsettle the bells.

There was the Sleeper. The Sleeper had a round white head and took slow, labored breaths through her nose. We were reminded of snoring. The shop filled with the Sleeper's slow breaths whenever she bent to her box.

There was Tim Pease. I sometimes thought of Tim Pease as a good model for the historical Jesus. He had very long hair, like the Jesus of standard depiction, but deep black and Semitically curled. On a subconscious level, the Jesus/Pease link may have drawn on the way the latter man walked, looking forward and keeping his hands at his sides and lifting his feet from the floor. Never varying his pace. The walk seemed to me quiet, essential. It seemed free of all personal foible.

There were a few drug dealers. This was according to Claude, who liked drugs and liked to imagine them in the more airy of the boxes in the shipment each day, the ones that would float when you tossed them.

And there was Clark Minds. Clark Minds didn't always have problems. Sometimes he'd stop at the counter for nothing more than a moment's talk. These moments could be difficult for Thompson Leach. Technically he'd have nothing to object to.

"It's an extremely cold day," Clark Minds might remark, grimacing, risking eye contact.

Thompson Leach would hold still.

"Good thing we don't live too far, Clark," I might say, running mail through the meter.

Eventually Clark Minds would say, "Yes."

He started telling us about his apartment during the short, brutal days of late January. I'd never been in Clark Minds' apartment. But I assumed that like mine it had a false latticed ceiling of yellowed styrofoam, covering who knows what, and a phone through which the all-purpose cheer of our landlord, Troy Nagurney, could be heard.

Troy Nagurney owned the building. He was part-owner of the postal shop too, which meant he both gave and took from me. "Is that right?" Troy Nagurney said to me when I informed him of this little irony. It was Troy Nagurney's favorite thing to say—'Is that right?' He'd say it as if he was really interested—in the subject, in you— which was almost never the case. I had to admire him for such basic insincerity. I connected it to his economic weight.

Clark Minds said that something unfortunate was beginning to take place in his apartment. He appeared stricken and shamed. Certain items had been moved from their places, he said. I wasn't sure how to respond.

"What items?"

Clark Minds grimaced. "Cat," he said finally.

"Cat," I repeated.

"Glass cat. Black cat. It's yawning."

"It's been moved?"

Clark Minds closed his eyes. "Turned around."

"I see," I said. "What else?"

Clark Minds spoke of other feathery events, explanation for which could probably be found in Clark Minds himself, as I tried saying.

A wing chair had been shifted a number of degrees. Some wouldn't have noticed, but he had. A coat had been moved from one peg to another. A book had been drawn partway out.

"Clark Minds was in earlier," I told Thompson Leach when he returned. I'll admit that I sort of enjoyed the effect that Clark Minds had on him.

Thompson Leach didn't answer.

"Says stuff has been moved in his apartment and there's no accounting for it."

Thompson Leach would not be riled. "Does he?" is all he would say.

This continued. A calendar switched months on Clark Minds. Items jumped shelves in the fridge. Knick-knacks appeared to the left of their spots, or to the right. If he'd chosen to tell you about this, you might not have understood well. Still, you'd have gotten the picture. He did not know the meaning of what was happening in his life. He feared that the force or forces at work would not be easily satisfied.

"The doorway," he said miserably one afternoon in a voice that was nearly beneath hearing.

I said, "The doorway, Clark?"

"Watch it?"

"Watch the doorway?"

"Yes."

"Watch the doorway. Why?"

He whispered with closed eyes, "I have to go out."

The doorway to the stairs that led to our apartments could be seen, at least partially, through storefront glass. He was asking me to note whether anyone went up to move things while he was out.

I gave him the okay sign. I wasn't at liberty to do as he wished (and couldn't have seen enough anyway); I just figured it might be good for Clark Minds to believe that no shadowy figures had been up the stairs in the time of his absence. It might help him be rational.

"No one," I therefore said to him, as soon as he got back.

Clark Minds left but returned minutes later and stared at me from the other side of the room.

I was busy at the time. I was tending shop by myself and couldn't help him. Customers noticed the cold and meaningful stare that was being directed at me by the short and wrong-looking man. It was embarrassing.

I went around the counter after everyone left. "Listen, Clark, you can't do that," I told him.

Just then Thompson Leach returned, setting off bells. He glanced at the two of us standing there. He glanced at us again. To me he nodded, lifting his chin. To Clark he said, "Leaving?"

He went into the back room.

"You have to realize—" I started again, but Clark Minds wasn't listening.

"*Chairs*," he mouthed.

"Look, Clark—"

"*Chairs.*"

I told Clark we could maybe finish the conversation later. More people had come in.

"So what was all that about?" Thompson Leach asked a while later. He was sorting some papers.

I just sighed.

He glanced at me, seemed to be waiting for more.

"Clark's demons," I told him.

"Ah."

When I told Clark Minds we could finish our conversation later, I meant outside the shop. And I said that. I told him I'd stop by his place after work.

Of course I forgot.

He returned three days later. It was the type of mid-winter day I remember from that time. Lunar and still. Outside, you couldn't hear much but the squeak of your steps in packed snow. The sound traveled your bones.

Clark made for his box. He 'trudged,' I'd have to say. He leaned forward. He didn't look at us, or stop to pull back his hood. He just went to his box and looked inside and turned and went back out.

A few of us were on at the time—me and Nina, Thompson Leach. Nobody spoke.

For me personally, the end of this story arrived without warning.

I ran out to the street one white evening, having locked myself out of my place. My cell had run down, and I was thinking about phone booths, wondering if maybe I'd seen one nearby. But I had some good fortune:

Thompson Leach had worked late. He was just leaving. I asked to use the shop phone. When I said who I was calling—Troy Nagurney—and said why, he showed me the keys on his ring. He shook them. "Got you covered," he said.

I invited Thompson Leach in.

It was warm in my apartment. I opened the front windows. Heat from the iron radiator buckled our lamplit view of the snow.

"Beer or something?" I asked my guest.

"Beer?" he responded. "Sure." He'd found my guitar.

When I returned, he was playing it. I could see that his technique was good, clearly a lot better than mine.

"Do you know Tara Johnson?" he asked.

"Tara Johnson," I said. "Does she live over that big laundry place?"

He said, "Yeah."

"I know who she is."

Thompson Leach was still smiling in reference to Tara Johnson. But since I wasn't personally acquainted with her—so he seemed to decide—there was no point in going on.

He kept playing. He played the first part of Nirvana's "Polly." It was a pretty good imitation.

After a while I got tired of watching him. I brought up Clark Minds, asked what he made of that whole situation. I expected to see his face crease with intolerance, I suppose. Instead he giggled.

I blinked up.

He stopped playing. "Things move around every time Clark goes out," he said softly.

I wish I could get you to see the exact look in his eyes. The pure and tender light. The warm press of sustaining vision. He seemed on the verge of telling me something huge, a thing that might change the whole tone of our relationship as manager and clerk. He seemed to be waiting, looking for some small sign, some gesture of affinity between us. On instinct, I withheld it.

I went over to see Clark Minds not long after Thompson Leach left. Whatever suspicions I may have been having by then, I was totally shocked.

Every chair in the room had been set on its side or turned over. Clean dishes—saucers and cups—had been placed here and there on the floor. A framed picture hung sideways. A big Oriental rug bellied down from the ceiling, to which it had been nailed.

Clark sat on a table. He stared at me much as he had a week earlier, the last time we'd spoken. He looked terrible. He looked righteous.

"Clark," I said. "Clark. You're being fucked with, Clark."

I waited before telling him though.

I looked at the saucers and cake plates and such, which seemed to have been spaced in such a way as to carry mysterious meaning. I looked at the chairs. I wondered at Thompson Leach, at his care, at the profound understanding of Clark Minds so evident in his project of loathing.

But I hesitated for a different reason. I hesitated in order to thrill at the specific, small weight of this moment in my life.

I'd have to find a new job. I'd have to find a new apartment.

I looked out at the flying snow.

What choice was there? It was time.

SAY MY NAME

The sex had been artless and rushed, like drinking down water. But she didn't seem to hold it against him.

Her hair was a little redder than he'd thought and wild in the morning humidity. She searched the ground floor of the time-share for her purse. The purse might have been left, she thought, in a room whose door was now closed—one of the rooms where people lay sleeping.

Everyone was sleeping.

Is there anything in the kitchen? she asked.

She was going through a pile of sweaters and coats on a chair. It was strange to him, and enjoyable enough—her idea that they were in this together.

She said, Fucking A.

He asked, What do you need out of it?

My smokes.

Get you a pack in town.

My shades.

Get some of those too.

He listened to himself as he said this.

She found the small purse on top of a bunch of shoes on the floor in the pantry. They walked to a diner.

The waitress didn't look at them but left a glass ashtray as she passed. It spun and made a singing sound as it wobbled to rest on the counter.

Sharilyn, his companion said to him. This was her name. He said it, but wrong.

She opened her mouth. Inside it, smoke nearly held still. Sharilyn, she pronounced.

Sharilyn, he repeated.

He wasn't hungry but ordered a roll.

When they returned, the people he'd come with— his friends—were awake and looking at the woman and him. He hadn't removed his shades.

Morning, they told him.

Hey, he responded.

He didn't know what they were thinking about him. He was thinking they were thinking something about him, and he was pleased. It was as if he was still drunk.

ADVENT SANTA

On the Wednesday before my kid's holiday break, school let out two hours early. I wasn't able to pick him up; I'd gotten some temp work that week. So I called my ex-girlfriend, Anne. Ben liked her a lot. When I returned, they were wrapped in twin afghans, Ben with his fingertips poked through the holes. They were couch-bound and watching the Ghost of Christmas Future refuse to say anything to the man in the nightgown and cap.

In a rush I called thanks. Anne shooed my word away with her hand.

"Does this actually happen?" said Ben.

She said, "Wait."

"I mean is he dead?"

"Just watch."

"Spirit!" the old man cried.

I ran water—for dishes. Then I stood waiting there, at the sink, at the window whose old wooden frame needed paint. In the yard, the dusk hour was on. Blue afterlight buried the leaves in the grass and managed even to pretty up the lighted plastic Santa deal, which was anchored with sand from the bed of my truck, and which this—what I'm telling—is about.

Because what happened next:

A vehicle stopped in the road. A teenager got out and took it—took the large Santa.

It was, I maybe should say, not worth much, and not really ours. A week earlier, Ben had come across it wrapped in tarp in the shed that was filled with stuff discarded by previous tenants, and had said, "He's the same, he's the one from my Advent calendar. Look."

Both faces were undetailed, both right-hand mittens lifted out and spread in cheery hellos.

So I told him, "All right," and picked the thing up— it was cracked on one side—and got Ben started on wiping it down while I went for an outdoor cord and a forty-pound bag of sand.

Because of the crack that ran to the hole in the base, that bag just fit. Because of the crack that ran to the hole in the base, this boy who'd entered the yard was now able to free the Santa just by tipping him as he pulled.

I cursed. I ran, threw open the door, then swung back around for my keys.

"What is it?" called Anne.

But I wouldn't say anything: I was not going to take what was happening here, not going to give it the firmness I knew it would have if I put it in words.

I jumped in my truck, jabbed the ignition. The boys—there were two—had an open Jeep. When they saw me behind them, their taillights shook, but the vehicle stabilized right away, even while picking up speed. They had the head and chest and lifted arm of the Advent Santa through the roll ball on the driver's side. The thief—if the thief was not the one driving—had hold of the base by the cord. But the base blew around.

When the boys took a left—without slowing—the shadowed bulk of Ben's Santa Claus tore free and smashed down on the pavement.

To keep from running it over, I had to lean sideways, yanking the wheel.

I was still on them. I got myself close enough to count bolt holes in the spare.

The road that the boys had turned onto is the road leading out of our neighborhood. And the road that we were all coming to next is a big one.

I saw the red light.

The boys flew into the intersection on faith, and something preserved them. They crossed four lanes of open traffic almost like they'd never been there, like they were just one of the twilight shadows racing the orderly grid. I couldn't do that. I couldn't blaze into that road without slowing to see what was in it. I gunned the truck to loop around some blooming lights in the first two lanes, then braked and sharpened the cut of my wheels to keep from hitting a speeding car in the final northbound lane. This swung me around. I twirled. For what seemed a long time, I waited for how things would be.

Nothing happened. Cars stopped in a blaring of sound and light before I was hit.

Waiting for me to right myself, though, was a cop. He never even put on his siren—just set his top lights running.

I rolled down my window. "Red Jeep," I was trying to say. "Did you see it?"

I was still catching my breath; the cop asked how

much I'd been drinking.

I said, "No—red Jeep. Two boys. They were trying to steal my kid's Santa."

The cop kind of studied me.

"DDJ or DOJ," I went on. "That's the plate. You could run it. DDJ, I think. For a red Jeep."

The cop asked to see my license, my registration and proof of insurance. I let my eyes close.

"Do you know what you just did?" the cop asked.

"They took my kid's Santa. His yard . . . decor."

"Failure to stop at a red light."

"He doesn't have much."

The cop spoke quietly. "Speeding. Reckless endangerment."

Again my heart was banging.

I sat with my knuckle bones hung to the wheel while the cop ran my plate in the squad car. I waited a long time. Fine snow had started to pour from the sky in the last of the light.

The cop gave me a break—one ticket: the failure to stop. Still, the fine was probably going to wipe out my earnings that day. I drove back slowly. I looked for the Santa Claus, wasn't too shocked not to find him. Once I was nearing my place again, though, I peered: I could make out a glow.

Anne and Ben had retrieved it somehow—the Santa. Its plastic back was cracked in, which meant that it wouldn't stand anymore; still, they had hooked up the power.

When I rose from the truck, we all looked at one another—Anne, my kid and me. No one knew how to

act—what to wonder or ask about first. In Anne's face—
in her eyes—I saw more of her than could have been
sorted out. All the trouble and tenderness. All together in
there, on hold. She'd opened one glove by her hip: knit
glove—with a coating of snowflakes.

"Guys tried to steal him," I began.

"What happened, Dad? What'd you do?"

I gave an account. I was looking at Ben, and at Anne,
who seemed like she could have had questions.

But for now she didn't ask them.

"We found him," Ben explained. "We tied him on
top of Anne's car."

I said, "Good. That's good."

And I nodded. And Anne pushed some snow from
her nose.

And it might have been one of those times—one of
those moments in holiday tales—where good things
happen for those who are good or have faith. Except
nothing happened at all. Anne stood in the yard in her
coat and her gloves. My kid horsed around in the snow.
The Santa Claus, laid on his back, on his hip, still raised a
lit mitten, like he was upset, maybe trying to free himself
from the twine he'd been tied to Anne's car with.

"He looks a little ridiculous," I mentioned.

Anne nodded. "Yes."

And then I was thinking: how dark, how late it was.
How swirled with the coldness of snow. I saw I could
maybe just do something here—something to get us
inside.

SOFA

A man once gave them a clean new sofa. "If you can use it, it's yours," he said. Her son, Terry, was pleased. The new furnishing was more comfortable than anything else they'd acquired. But then the man, who lived in a larger house across the street, fell into the habit of dropping by. He'd relax on the sofa he'd given them, stretch his legs, cross his ankles, swing his feet. "He's all right," her son tried to say about the man. "You," she said. "You're all right." He was fourteen and had sweet green eyes and hard shoulders he showed by cutting his shirtsleeves off. When he found that she'd given the sofa to Goodwill, he wouldn't talk to her. He was in the dark, playing video games. Clean glasses were there in the wire dish drainer, but she leaned to the sink and pulled out the sprayer and drew her face all the way down to one side and filled her cheek with water.

ABOUT ME AND MY COUSIN

Country Music

We were hardly ten minutes out of that place when my cousin said, Shit, we need gas. We stopped at a Shell. It had sixteen pumps beneath a giant white ceiling but no one was there. Hidden radio played. I can't hold you like I want to, came the teeny sad voice from a long time before. I walked toward the road. The electrical poles were like spindles. Like stakes. They'd been driven through edges of a massive heaving sky.

Hidden Radio

In that house was a carpeted dining room. Into its longest wall my cousin's dead father had built low cabinets with sliding doors made of dark veneer paneling. The doors were moved by recessed pulls which were round, like golden coins, but I couldn't touch them; I wasn't allowed to go in. My cousin would switch his flashlight on, close the doors against me, then work the scored dials that controlled the tuning and volume on a portable radio. Loud static had meaning: my cousin had left the physical space of his father's cabinets. My cousin was loose. He could be in the room, next to me, a specter. He could be moving in time. It was a fine ploy. Since I wasn't allowed to go in, I couldn't ever verify that my cousin had not in fact flown.

My Cousin's Dead Father

They must have had decent drugs to give out at the Dickinson County emergency room. He was in high spirits. He wore drawstring bathing trunks and an off-white porkpie hat and his belly was round. The hair on it had a gold sheen. Since the thumb had been lost in the wheel of the hoist for the boat, he thought we should dive in that place. The water was green and dim near the bottom. Rocks glowed. Lengths of seaweed caressed our thin legs. I'd burst to the surface, blinded and scared, then see the white flash of the cast on his arm. No one had gotten to sign it yet; we had to retrieve the thumb first.

Bottom

The summer my cousin stayed with us, I switched beds. Normally I slept in the bottom bunk, which offered a nice enclosed feeling. But I switched to the top. My cousin, I knew, would prefer that one. I wanted him to see that here in this place my whims, and not his, would come first.

Beds

I woke to the sounds of my cousin banging someone in the other bed. I was in a hotel room. The air-conditioning unit was feeble; the air was stale. In the darkness I felt around for my pants and keys and got out of there. The night wasn't bad. It was cooler than the room had been. I sat in the car and turned the ignition in order to rocker my seat and bring down all the windows. Country music was on, then a deejay saying his piece for late drivers while they were in range.

AT THE BEACH HOTEL

We all thought my wife's sister was suffering. We were at the hotel, on the beach just south of Carmel, where we'd met for her daughter's wedding. She's a quiet person, my wife's sister. But at the beach hotel, we read her silence as having to do with Jeanine, her daughter's stepmother, a tall and flashy forty-something who'd taken charge of the plans, and with her ex-husband, Ted, who she hadn't seen much of in the years since he'd left for Jeanine.

We were out on the balcony, my wife, her sister and I. Brandon, my wife's fifteen-year-old cousin, lay on a floral bedspread in the formal gloom of the space behind us, watching cartoons with the volume down.

"Beautiful," said my wife, as if this was a fact she might like to contest.

My wife's sister nodded. She pulled her legs to her chest, shifted her cotton fleece throw.

I checked my messages, then leaned to the balcony rail and tried to attend the screech of the gulls, the swell of the vast gray water.

"You know Jay used to live out here," my wife said to her sister.

I nodded. "North of here. I lived in Santa Cruz."

My wife's sister then turned her face toward me out of courtesy, and I saw my wife's intent: for me to provide the distraction of stories from my own doomed early life.

How I'd dropped out of college. Gone West. Hitchhiked the coast. Found work as a chimney sweep. Got married to a girl who answered the phone for a veterinarian. Lived with her and a dozen stray cats in a teensy one-bedroom house.

My wife's sister chuckled.

"The girl I was married to—Maura was her name— wanted a garden. There wasn't room for a garden. There was no grass. But the landlord said he'd consider taking out the concrete courtyard and putting in sod. So then at one point he heard there was free soil to be had. Some friend of his had soil in a dump truck. They talked, and the truck showed up one day and the load was dumped in the courtyard. So instead of a courtyard there was now a small mountain of dirt, which the landlord never did anything about, of course. A tree grew out of it after a while. A big twisting weed tree."

We all laughed quietly.

"On hot afternoons its pods would crack open. Shoot little seeds at the windows."

That night, after the rehearsal dinner, I smoked pot with my wife's cousin, Brandon. We stood in the parking lot. Pain, dull and steady, had claimed my left hip; I'd forgotten to pack medication.

Soon afterward, I returned to the balcony and was surprised to run into my wife's sister.

"Nice night," I think I said.

She nodded.

A moon had come up. When the breeze fell away, the air was a mild balm of salt. We watched the mirrory waters slip down the sand toward the break of the waves. For a while we did this, not thinking to talk.

I didn't know where Maura lived.

I didn't know what she did for a living, whether she still got sand in the sheets or kissed with a peach-wine tongue.

I didn't know her middle name.

I couldn't say if her hair was still long—the honey-blonde tangle of unwashed curls which had crowded the blink of her eyes.

THE GOTH OF SECURITYONE FIELD

August 9, 2010

Harlan Cichowski
P.O. Box 1872
Culpepper, VA 22701

Brad Colliers
154 5th Avenue
Brooklyn, NY 11215

Dear Mr. Colliers:

I received your letter of July 17th and want first to offer apology for what must seem my delay in response.

Secondly—and with all due respect to you, sir—it's my feeling that you should probably be subjected to gentle admonishment. If really you are a baseball man, you must understand that I was neither "leader" nor "lynchpin" of the

'02 club. Thus I must take your saying so as: a) misplaced
courtesy; or b) a stab at flattery—which, I suppose, may well
have hit the mark with others, but not with me. I never
accepted about myself what statistics would have had me
believe, Mr. Colliers. Always I felt that I could do more (and
proved that, I think, in the summer and fall of '02, after the
Vargas trade gave me the chance to play every day). As of the
spring of '04, however, when injuries forced my retirement, I
gave no further resistance to the verdict already prepared: I'd
been a career backup, a lifetime .240 hitter on clubs that were
basically out of contention before the all-star break. I'd played
with great pride, and honorably, I hope, but without
distinction, unless one takes your view and tries to make
something of my having been the "only man to close a mitt"
on fastballs thrown by Osterbauer during an actual game.

Good luck with your book project, sir. Certainly his story is a
tragic one. Are you aware that when that plane went down
he'd probably thrown no more than 300 pitches in the major
leagues?

Good luck to you.

Harlan Cichowski

August 18, 2010

Harlan Cichowski
P.O. Box 1872
Culpepper, VA 22701

Brad Colliers
154 5th Avenue
Brooklyn, NY 11215

Dear Mr. Colliers:

You say that it's your "modest hope" that I will have no choice
but to admire your persistence. Is it not a question of where
persistence is applied?

By chance, however, you catch me during the cocktail hour,
which brings an infusion of violet to the hemlock woods.

Madison Osterbauer. No player will ever be as great as the one
from whom the chance to play is stolen at an early age. Is that
the story? I suppose it is. From the tone of your questions, I
infer, as well, an inclination to write a mystery book.

What might have caused the rookie "phenom"—the kid who
had, in a matter of weeks, "captured the imagination of fans
the world over"—to be so quietly discarded in a sudden off-
season trade? You have my interest there, Mr. Colliers. Perhaps
when you finally solve that one, you could spend some time
on my own. Why did they say that they loved me in
Pittsburgh?

One day I was part of their plans in Detroit, the next I was clearing my locker out. Why?

Forgive me. At the same time, let me be clear: if the legend of Madison Osterbauer has to be built out of smoke, you will, I'm afraid, be forced to rely on others.

You ask about the defacement of the locker-room wall, for example. Yes, this happened. No, we never learned why. No one confessed. No one, in fact, was accused.

If there's anything more to say on this subject, I'm not sure what that might be.

What I'll offer: realities.

On the first of September, 2002, at the time when rosters expanded, we were joined by three players from our triple-A club and one from double-A Springfield, Osterbauer being the double-A guy. You should understand something, Mr. Colliers: while it isn't unheard of—a September call-up coming from a double-A team—it isn't the norm, and there is in the clubhouse what I would call an unarticulated question: why, if the kid is so promising, has he lingered in double-A ball? What, in this particular player, is management so eager to behold?

These were the questions which underlay the experience of seeing him for the first time.

Let me ask you something: did you ever stand in the same

room with Madison Osterbauer? Television distances oddities, renders them small and safe. Did you see him in the flesh?

"Oh, no," was the reaction of a player with whom I'd roomed on the road. "You're kidding me. You are kidding me."

What we saw: rail-thin kid, about seven foot tall; barbell piercing the somewhat sore-looking skin of a sparse blond eyebrow; mess of dyed hair; unmissable darkness rimming the wets of his lower eyelids. And the trump card: black disc, like a plastic tartar-sauce cap, in the stretched-out meat of his earlobe.

In our own clubhouse we saw this.

Rather than pretend that nothing at all was happening, as others were, the guy with whom I'd roomed on the road—'Z,' let's say—proceeded to ask, "Is that painful?"

Osterbauer looked at him as if he didn't know what he meant.

"That?" said Z, allowing his fingertips to float toward the ear in question.

"Not at the moment," Osterbauer said.

"But it was?"

"Sort of."

"When you were doing it?"

"Yes."

Among the guys—all of whom had gone silent for this—Z
was well-known for the way that he laughed, blinking and
looking around in delight and surprise, spreading the feeling.

When he recovered, Z offered a firm right hand, and
Osterbauer told us his name.

~

You request my perspective on his greatness. As I believe I
indicated in my first letter, the boy threw only two hundred-
some pitches. He threw in fewer than ten games. And he
belongs, by your reckoning, with the all-time greats? There I
must disagree with you, sir.

As his catcher, I can say that he was talented, perhaps uniquely
so. His kick was so high and his pivot so quick that I never
really learned to expect the control he was able to achieve—
especially given the oft-noted movement on his fastball.

He was very talented. And I can say one thing more, in
relation to his famous third outing.

Although he'd acquitted himself well enough in his first two
outings, in middle relief, there were those on the team—and I
was one—who felt that the Skip was committing a kind of
travesty in sending him out as a closer in the Bronx. It wasn't

serious, I felt. It rubbed in our faces the fact that for us these games were meaningless; we were an act, an exhibition.

I expected failure. Not failure: bloodbath. Crucifixion. Something like that.

And when it didn't happen? When, as you say, he "razed in succession the heart of the Yankee order, leaving thousands agape …"?

Actually there are two things I would like to say about this. First, Osterbauer listened to me. I'd been in the majors since he was a child: he trusted the calls I signed him. Second, after he tossed those first three pitches and had himself stuck in a 3–0 hole, something happened. He changed. In the rising whirl of stadium seats, the Yankee fans seemed to think they smelled blood and were hooting, doing their best to raise a wild, delirious noise. I'd called for a fastball. The kid never nodded his head. He was shifting: every last trace of every last thought he'd had in the whole of his life was now leaving his body. It was as if I could see that somehow. He was elemental. He was clean. He was force.

~

I had it in mind to grant you the dusk hour, Mr. Colliers. It's full dark.

I hope some of this helps you.

Harlan Cichowski

September 1, 2010

Harlan Cichowski
P.O. Box 1872
Culpepper, VA 22701

Brad Colliers
154 5th Avenue
Brooklyn, NY 11215

Dear Mr. Colliers:

Once more will I sit with you for a time, as long as we're clear
on the terms: in no way will I thus consider myself obliged to
respond to each or any of the questions you've sent my way.

Eight years ago—the year after the attacks. September '02.

I wasn't alone in having trouble believing the speed and
magnitude of what happened in the aftermath of the outing
at Yankee Stadium. Suddenly we had fans—enthusiasts at the
airport, many lifting handmade signs. Suddenly we had
crowds. Bedsheet banners hung from the decks at
SecurityOne.

THE GOTH'S GALLERY
WE LOVE YOUR M.O., M.O.

I remember watching a screen in the clubhouse after the kid's
next save. It was Stuart Scott—SportsCenter. It was the top of
the show.

"Who's next to get scorched by the Goth?" he cried.

A group of us stood there watching this, and not a single person could speak.

We were a last-place team, Mr. Colliers. We hadn't been given prominent mention on television for as long as I'd been there.

You ask if there was resentment.

No. Not if I understand your question. Modern-day ballplayers are happy enough to be playing in the relative light.

There wasn't resentment. At the same time, the experience was strange. What might have seemed novel and interesting to readers of the American sports page was different for us in the clubhouse. It was real. A plain truth of our days.

Let me jump back to before that time when the circus came to town: Osterbauer's first outing. Two innings of middle relief. If you're writing an actual book about this, I'm sure you know his line. One hit, two walks, and a run, with a couple of K's? Something like that. Not amazing. Not bad. And afterward, as per custom, we razzed him, a group of us did. Player O lay a slugger's arm around the kid's pale shoulders and said, "Well well," and we laughed uproariously as he continued: "Is that some fearsome fastball he got or is that some fearsome fastball?" We rejoined, "Yeah!" "Mr. Fearsome," Player O said, and we laughed. "Mr. Fearsome!" we cried. O said, "With the hair." "The hair and jewelry!" cried

Z. "We got something to go with that jewelry?" asked O. "The pretty jewelry?" "Oh yeah!" a few of us called. And Z, who was so overcome that he'd let himself sag to a knee on the floor, produced nail polish, purple with flecks. "Oh!" we said, "Oh!" trying to breathe, as the kid was lowered into his chair and purple enamel was neatly applied to the nails of his non-pitching hand.

I was wiping my tears.

When I looked at his face to gauge his reaction, however, the wind left my sails. Osterbauer wasn't there. Osterbauer was miles from us. It was as if he'd been able to push pause on himself; what we had was his skinny, limp frame.

But that isn't quite right. He wasn't miles from us. He was present, observing the raucous display in some sense; he was just out of reach.

And what did he think?

What does a person like that think, Mr. Colliers?

I stared at him, my silence beginning to affect the others, whose laughter had flagged.

I looked at his skin, which was paler than other skin. I looked at his eyes, which were larger than other eyes. I looked at his hair, which was doll-like, brittle. I looked at his ear.

~

I understand that your job, as a popular historian, is to enchant. Even so, I leave you with this thought, Mr. Colliers: in '02, Madison Osterbauer wasn't some figure from the Brothers Grimm. We'd welcomed this person into our house. He lived with us. He ate at our table.

I bid you a good night, sir,

Harlan Cichowski

September 11, 2010

Harlan Cichowski
P.O. Box 1872
Culpepper, VA 22701

Brad Colliers
154 5th Avenue
Brooklyn, NY 11215

Dear Mr. Colliers:

Either you lack all power of inference or you choose to be
dense in order to elicit response. I don't like being toyed with,
Mr. Colliers.

No, I was not comfortable with Osterbauer—
"interpersonally," as you say. I wasn't, and I don't think many
of us were. When you go into battle with someone, there has
to be a level of security.

Yes, the issue of the defacement of the locker-room wall may
have fomented mistrust of the young hurler. Shortly
afterward, however, he spoke to us, unbidden. He denied
involvement; as far as I know, he was not disbelieved.

This will be our final communication. I'm sorry to abandon
delicacy, but I need you to understand me: do not write back.

Sincerely,
Harlan Cichowski

April 4, 2011

Harlan Cichowski
P.O. Box 1872
Culpepper, VA 22701

Brad Colliers
154 5th Avenue
Brooklyn, NY 11215

Dear Mr. Colliers:

I made one mistake. I didn't jettison either of the letters which arrived bearing your name and address. I didn't open them, but I didn't throw them away.

There comes a time when one is led to consider the meaning of choices made.

How to start?

Perhaps with a memory: a home game, vs. the Devil Rays— another pennywise outfit playing, at that point, only for pride.

Some days you look out through the bowl to the sky and see the procession of milky fat clouds, and you lose gravity. The real slowness of things all across the wide prairie makes itself known to you.

In the top of the eighth of that lukewarm affair, we were up by a couple of runs. A rookie—Jackson? Jackman?—stepped to the plate against Osterbauer. Small, right-handed hitter. Overmatched but unafraid. He'd fallen behind in the count, 0–2. But he couldn't be lured into swinging at borderline stuff, and so had my respect.

When the count had gone full, I called for the heat. Up and in. Corner of the zone. Osterbauer nodded; I shifted in order to show both him and the ump the bull's-eye.

The rookie—Jackson, Jackman—could do nothing with this pitch. Still, he got around on the ball and fouled it back over home plate.

This next part, Mr. Colliers, is why I remember, why I'll never forget.

As Osterbauer had hit my target exactly, I called again for that pitch—fastball, up and in. Again the kid nodded. Again the rookie swung and fouled it back over home plate. Now I signed change-up, which the rookie hadn't yet seen. Osterbauer, however, shook me off, wanted fastball again.

All right, I pronounced in silence as once more I shifted my mitt.

Eight times Madison Osterbauer threw the exact same pitch. Seven times the young hitter—Jackson, Jackman—swung and fouled it off. I mean to say: the *same pitch*. I had the best seat in the house, and I'm telling you: that pitch crossed the plate at the same angle, the same speed, the same place, within millimeters.

It was uncanny.

Upon his eighth and final swing, the rookie got nothing but stadium breeze. Was he tired? Had he suspected futility and so lost a small measure of sharpness? Whatever the case, he failed—just barely—to get his hands high enough. We left him standing there—Jackson, Jackman—collecting his twisted parts.

~

Please believe that I ask what I ask without rancor: what would you like to conclude?

I ask in all honesty.

If you knew everything you wanted to know about the incident of the mark on the locker-room wall, would you try to persuade your readers that management was scared? Would you hold that such fear was the principal cause of Osterbauer's being traded? Would you argue that, had it not been for the trade, he wouldn't have boarded that flight?

As weak as the lines of the argument seem, I do feel curiously prone to them now. Each atom of chance and circumstance that allowed for the player's untimely death begins to compel regret.

If he hadn't played baseball . . .

If he hadn't cast doubt on himself . . .

If management hadn't drafted him, or hadn't decided to call him up until spring of the following year . . .

~

A few facts:

1.   It was not a swastika.
2.   It was not obscene, if this is what some would suggest by calling it "art of the men's room."
3.   In the aftermath, no direct pressure was placed upon Osterbauer or anyone else.

At this point, I might as well offer you more on that last one, Mr. Colliers.

The Skip called us and the coaches together on a Sunday prior to a game. He'd already met with others, he explained. Now he was meeting with us. "If anyone knows anything . . ." he began. "About that . . ." And without turning, he flipped his arm toward the mark on the wall behind him.

He appeared reduced, ashamed to be talking about this. He never once looked at the mark on the wall—which in fact was an 'X' in black paint. We didn't look either. We'd seen it upon our arrival, felt it as a slap in the face.

"If anyone knows anything," the Skip said simply, "I need to know what you know."

And this would have been the end of the meeting if

Osterbauer—whom we'd given a few yards of clearance—had not then spoken. "I need to say something, I think." The rookie pitcher's voice was firm, but his elbow appeared to be shaking. "I haven't been here that long. You don't know me well yet. But I don't paint. I'm not a painter ... I'm not a liar."

By the last words, his shaking had become so pronounced that his words wobbled out like a top.

The Skip looked pained and mumbled something about nobody being accused. I was blinking at Osterbauer. With others, he'd turned away. The team had begun to disperse.

~

If he'd been less silent, less of a question mark ...

If he'd been traded a couple days earlier ...

If his alarm clock had failed, or if he'd slept through it, missing the scheduled flight ...

But of course, this is pointless. What happened happened. Osterbauer was who he was.

~

Perhaps there were those who could say about him, Well, he's a rookie. Well, he's just shy. Well, he's a colorful character. Most of us, however, had eyes, Mr. Colliers. Most of us were in the habit of using them. I remember one overnight flight,

the cabin in darkness. I was returning from the john. The
rookie reliever's sleeping face glowed in the light he'd been
reading by, and there, in the still-living flesh of his ear, was the
blackness. In the aisle I stood staring.

If you forget, for a moment, how accustomed you are to
indulging the spirit of novelty, questions arise. Would you not
agree, Mr. Colliers? Though perhaps inchoate, they arise just
the same. For there must have been reasoning. Osterbauer
wasn't a burn victim. Fate had not stuck him with this.
Neither had he divided his corpus from ours by accident, as
one might pick a scab. There must have been reasoning.
There must have been consciousness, will. Follow this
thought, and you realize that you're coming to know more
about him—but also less. For really, who is he? You observe
the careful, still way he passes among you in the clubhouse.
You watch how he shifts, how he sidles, passing with
downcast eyes, and you begin to understand. Eventually
knowledge arrives. You see there is no definitive way to be
sure that he's not in fact hostile to you. You see there is no
dismissing a possibility: that this young man is an enemy to
all you believe in.

So the question of who did it—who chose to commit the act
of defacement in the SecurityOne locker room between 8:45
and a little past 10:15 on a Saturday night—this does not
interest me. Who perpetrated the offense? you want to know.
Who cares? For Osterbauer *could* have, you see? He could
have hopped into the car the evening before and taken that
road through the woods, the one so smooth in its curves as to
nearly induce sleep. He could have rolled into the lot and

stepped from the car and gone through the doors and purchased materials—evidence, technically, even though none would be found. The quart of black paint. All Surface Enamel, let us say. And the brush. A Wooster Pro, Mr. Colliers. Four and a half inches long.

He could have gone home. He could have then walked amongst us the next morning, nodding when nodded at, mouthing *hey*, concealing all the while a terrible wordless intention. Do you see, Mr. Colliers? This person— Osterbauer—he could have snuck in when the trainer was gone and wondered (strange that he hadn't before) just what he meant to inscribe.

A word? A symbol?

No, a scourge, in the end: an expression of hand, full-felt in the rush of its moment: a general blotting out—crossed stabs of controversion. Osterbauer could have. The Wooster then loose in the palm. The black drips making their way to that floor like a kind of alien blood. It was in the kid's nature. Was it not? It was in the kid's soul, whose true essence would now be revealed.

For the last time, good luck.

Harlan Cichowski

DESULTORY

For a time I wrote and reported the news for a paper in South Dakota. I lived in a furnished apartment with several lamps and no overhead lights, and I slept on the couch, in the twined subsidence of passing cars and a pivoting fan.

The big story: the heat.

It cooked the oily nubbery of that couch, which glowed like a penny. It slicked my ribs and shoulder blades, sometimes producing fat trickle.

I disliked writing the story of heat, lodged as it was in the reasonable voices of men from the National Weather Service, from Water and Power and Light. That story was dull. It seemed blatantly counterfeit. But on days when the heat finally brought someone down, I disliked writing it more.

An old man with frayed lips and thin arms in the knot of a T-shirt he never got off.

Or that's how I saw it.

I typed the man's name.

I decided I smoked. I knew nobody in that place. No one could tell me I didn't.

I chose Winston Lights. And I chose my provider of

them, a convenience-store clerk named Melissa.

Of course we were trapped—she in a yieldless two-tone shirt with her name pinned over the pocket; I in my education.

But I wormed out my sign. I left my right hand on the counter, and shifted, from nerves, one finger. I looked at the back of her neck long enough to be seen.

Red blemishes. Bones. A fine hair.

One night I dumped ice in the clawfoot tub and woke my dormant genes.

One night I discovered a glitch in my skin. In my face. I pressed my thumbnail in, thinking to make it a scar.

I had one ally—a staff photographer. He was quiet but smiled dynamically, as if he might break out in laughter.

We drove, he and I, to a nursing home in the middle of the great, baking plain. This low, exposed box. Its central AC threw a deep and malevolent hum.

We'd come for a birthday. The oldest woman around. The oldest woman on Earth, just about. This was our story to tell.

Actually it was her story, but the woman was comatose. The woman had flown—and why not? She lived in a closet, behind a blue thickness of glass, in the ticking of an antique clock.

A nurse said, Used to be an old diary here.

She said it apologetically, as if I might have interviewed that.

But the photographer scored. We received top billing

in LIFE & STYLE, above the fold. South Dakotans could read the woman's lined face and think that they saw, in the light on her eye, serenity and wisdom.

I put a block of ice in a pan and slept by it on the floor.

I leaned my car to the jostling rubble. The car's AC was on the fritz and I was feeling not well—like the lobes of my brain had unfolded in flower.

Even at full acuity, though, I was pressed. The road would flutter away in liquid silver visions.

Come out with me, I think I said.

What? said the girl named Melissa.

But she reconsidered. She let her question expire.

Winston Lights, she said to me.

Yes! I responded. Yes!

My summer's highlight, this probably was. The highlight of my year.

That's to say, our date paled.

She and I and two of her friends—both of them, strangely, named Mike—went out to the bar of a restaurant that made a display of ads of yesteryear. The Twins were on TV. One of the Mikes watched the Twins. The other, whose mustache had never been shaved—so downy and light, it seemed—talked without tiring, talked without cease.

Later, in the dark of their rental's front yard, Melissa climbed a tree.

I thought many things. That she knew what I wanted with her. That she knew we had not much to say. That the way she was laughing, up there in the tree, was self-conscious, untried—something new for her: a laughter she maybe had the idea would translate to whatever I spoke.

I couldn't sleep.

I drank too much and passed out with a pizza heating in the oven.

Then woke up in shock. I couldn't get air. I climbed to the roof, hung over the peak.

Smoke from the various window holes rose past me, toward the stars. A zillion hidden insects shaped a lush and melting sound. I lay there and breathed. I allowed the left half of my face to take the coarse print of the shingle.

Was it the next day, when the photographer came looking for me?

The air was heavy and more or less still. The photographer called my name.

He looked in the bedroom, probably taking in the olden glow of bedposts.

I don't sleep there, I called.

Why's that? came his voice.

I just don't, I called back. Too hot.

But it wasn't the truth. The truth, in likelihood? That bed had a spot like a bruise on a pear. In that bed some lone person had died.

THE FIFTY

My uncle stopped me in the hallway and showed me a fifty. He nodded. Take it. I did, then waited through what he'd just purchased the right to say next.

Later I was shooting baskets. He walked out, put up his hands. But instead of shooting he rolled the ball away and pulled up the front of his shirt.

Hit me.

I looked at him.

Go on. Hard as you can.

I tried laughing.

Hit me. It won't hurt.

He feigned with his open right hand. I flinched. He rushed me, then laughed as I tried to back my way out of the lock of his arm. He'd been in drug treatment. His wife had taken his kids. He was bankrupt. His throat had spots.

Easy there. Easy. He lifted both arms. He was laughing.

I stared at him.

Easy there, tiger.

I said I was going inside.

At dinner I saw that my mother had placed him across from me at the table.

Where's your fifty?

What?

That fifty I gave you. Where is it?

I'd slipped it, folded, into a back pocket, the left. I checked it now.

You've got to learn to be more careful with your money. Look what I found in the driveway.

Everyone was watching. My mother was trying to smile. My uncle held the folded bill and gave it an expert shake, like he might have done to extinguish a match.

ACQUIRED FROM EX-GIRLFRIENDS

1.

Cheap leather coat K's father lent me when we were visiting and the weather turned cold. It had belonged to his brother, a cop, but had never been worn because the brother, as K's father explained, died within a month of their getting back from Mexico, where it had been bought. K looked tired when I slipped the thing on—sheeny brown, belted, lapelled. "It fits," I said, smiling. She was looking out the window at the sleet, as if she was no longer interested in me. This was not so. Who would be snuck down the hall to her little-girl bedroom later that night?

2.

Hoop earrings, gold, which S removed for safekeeping the night we pitched my tent at a rest stop off I-80, I think in the state of Illinois. Later, with A, I found them in one of the mesh bags hanging inside the tent. We were camping outside Houston while we looked for an apartment. It was summer and hot. I considered leaving the earrings there in hopes of A discovering them and having to value me more. They called to me, though. I licked them and wiped them in my shirt. I worked them into a pair of ridge piercings.

3.

A 1953 Vassar College yearbook, heavy as stone. Among the sophomores, on page 108, N's grandmother appears. She's a beauty, as N used to like to point out: the long neck, not sloping from the vertical; the small lips—subtle conductors, they seem, of all sorts of unconfessed life. Sometimes I turn to that page and feel dwarfed by the history. How many years of privilege and breeding were amassed in the making of this girl? How many more would be put into the making of N, a beautiful girl in her own right, though afflicted with stances and moods?

4.

Rubber-soled corduroy slippers, size ten, which C used to leave by the door of her hut near the beach in Santa Cruz. "You're supposed to leave work boots out, aren't you?" I said. "Something more menacing?" C laughed, which she didn't do often enough for somebody who was lighthearted. "Are people supposed to picture bald shins?" I went on. "He might beat them with the

morning paper? Is that it?" We laughed. Then I started
wearing the slippers around. They're burgundy. They fit.

5.

A waterstained paperbound copy of Weber's *Protestant
Ethic and the Spirit of Capitalism*, which O read in her
first year of grad school. For a while I resented in O many
things, among them her foresight in removing little by
little, over a span of days, all that she knew she wouldn't
want to have to go back to my place for later. But she
missed something. Weber. I flip through its pages and
here is her hand—its gentle, unclosed *a*'s and *o*'s. Here is
her voice. *Credit =Worthiness. Environment? Annoying!
Power of church.*

GREATMAN AND THE NON-HUMAN GIRL

When Greatman lost his powers, he got depressed. Depression was natural, he supposed. In a case like his— a singular case—depression was to be expected. So Greatman gave in. Depression had for him a novelty. When he woke, it was there for him—the meaning of light in his hanging gray clothes, waiting to be assumed, like the clothes themselves, except that he felt like he wore his own body, a coarse, ripped suit whose fabrics would flap in the stillness of dawn.

That's when he went walking.

The sound of his heels on the paving stones was the beat of a tale whose language accrued: taut codes of graffiti monikers. Padlocked roller doors. But no one was listening; nobody would hear of this time.

Greatman found a figurine. Brown dog snapped in two.

The strangest thing, and the saddest, perhaps: the name of the man he'd been when not being Greatman had fallen away. That man had known the Commissioner and consorted with Marla Stone. Had Greatman ever imagined this period of life—the time of his ruin—he might have believed he would simply retire as that man, whose panics gave rise to amusement, whose general secrecy, however odd, had given him minor pull.

But the man had been fiction. Greatman could see this now. The man's life: a footprint in water.

At home—a modest street-front apartment—he washed the ceramic pieces. He dried them in a towel. They were almost too small for his hands. When he joined them, however, their break disappeared within the gloss of a fine brown body.

He went out for glue.

On his return, in the fleet and amalgamatory dusk hour, he saw a café, and he paused and went in. He was aware of the privacy of those who sat reading at tables. He was aware of his age, its malleable print on his face. He was aware of the crackling weightlessness of the plastic bag holding the glue.

He said aloud, "I have secrets."

A young woman had come with his espresso.

"What are they worth anymore?" Greatman asked.

He blinked and looked into her face.

The young woman had set on his table a saucer whose innermost ring held the cup. Her eyes were a match for the beverage within—nearly black. Beneath each eye, a wrinkle extended the slant of the opposite eyebrow.

He said, "I saved every soul in this city. At least twice. I saved you."

"You saved me?"

"If you were here then."

"Why?"

"Why what?

"Why bother saving someone unless you're sure that's what they want?"

The question was flippant; Greatman watched her moving eyes to find its truth.

For a moment she turned away. "You want to hear mine?"

"Yours?"

"Secret?"

He nodded, just once.

"I'm not human. I was made on a production line, by a renegade corporation. They made women. For purposes of sex, of course. But I managed to make my escape."

"Go on."

The young woman laughed out loud.

While speaking, she'd leaned to the back of the opposite chair. Greatman made an attempt at reading the words tattooed in cursive across the cords that bulged in her wrists.

The discovery and subsequent mending of the small ceramic figurine brought purpose to Greatman's wanderings. He opened his eyes. In the watery light of morning suns that trembled in east-west corridors, things glinted. He took to wearing a child's rucksack to stow what he found.

A cabinet knob—pewter.

A herringbone wallet chain.

A single malachite bead.

A shot glass.

A key.

A locket.

Another key.

A pocked billiard ball, yellow, the nine.

A horse made of wire.

A plastic dancing girl.

A glass chess piece.

A tiepin.

A die.

His personal favorites: the ones like the figurine, requiring intervention.

He found a blue rhinestone. It was nearly perfect for the sightless fox in a small gold brooch. He lit off a firework in the vented chamber of tea infuser. The dent was blown round.

It struck Greatman that these small works of reclamation comprised an entity, but it was not one he could name. He liked to regard them. On the round of a coffee table, they cast sharp, parallel shadows. He saw these as turning, like hands of a clock—pointed hands.

Pocketknife. Bird call. Chalice.

Each had been lifted from blear and demise, restored to the science of light. And yet what could be seen, about any one of the items, was small in relation to what couldn't.

That's to say there were mysteries. Of use. Of provenance. Greatman felt the presence of such mysteries in his apartment. His rooms had new vitality. So when his mind fixed on the subject of the non-human girl—as it did, he realized, with some frequency—he was able to imagine asking her in without shame.

She might need refuge, he knew. He would tell her: she could hide here.

Though Greatman had felt ungrounded offering confessions to a total stranger, he saw that he had revealed less than had the young woman in the end. He had not, for example, spoken his name.

Perhaps this had been for a reason.

If he said who he was, if he voiced the name, *Greatman*, the non-human girl would be forced to compare its attendant lore of triumph with the person addressing her now.

He would be believed, or he would be disbelieved; either way he would come up for pity. And to imagine that outcome—his being pitied—was to see his own investment in possibilities of a different kind. This small hope: that by speaking openly, he might feel his expired glow.

Greatman stood up. He tucked a dollar bill under his saucer and turned toward the doors.

Twice more he had to return to the café before he caught sight of the non-human girl. She looked tired. Her lips were pale and dry. She looked like she didn't recognize him when she came with his saucered brew.

"I've been thinking—about what you said last time," he said.

In her face he saw minor disruption; he gave her a chance to recall.

"I can tell you," he said in his quietest voice. "I've had some experience in matters like this. To be a fugitive from the lawless is worse than being a fugitive from justice in one respect: the lawless will never give up. If you sense that the man who bought you, or agents of those who manufactured you—or anyone else—is getting closer, don't dismiss that. And if you need to erase your trail . . ." He leaned back, rolling his weight to a hip, taking from a pocket a manila card that he had prepared. "This is my address. I'm not the man I was, but I'll help in any way that I can."

She exclaimed softly, "Jesus fuck!"

Greatman turned. In a casual way, meant to encourage discretion, he extended his hand and took hold of his cup.

That night, for the first time in months, perhaps, he dreamed of his former life. He dreamed movement: his sailing over the tops of buildings in the midnight chill. That massive geometry, shifting, jeweled with light. All his—to behold, to keep.

The following night, he didn't dream, or dreamt blindly.

He was awakened by a sound at the door. Quickly he cinched the belt of his robe, not doubting the news that instinct conveyed: the non-human girl had arrived.

But Greatman was wrong. A dented beer can rolled in the wind that traveled his street.

He wondered why he had been sure it was she. He wondered if they were connected now, if the can, rolling to and fro in the dark, meant the non-human girl was in peril.

She appeared three nights later. Greatman had eaten

dinner, had washed his dishes and set them to dry. At his table he worked on a gyroscope. It was small, the diameter of a fifty-cent piece. The rotor on the central axis was loose, and Greatman hoped to secure it by fashioning stops of jewelry wire.

She was not alone.

Flanking her in the doorway were two young men. At first he thought that the taller of the boys had been hurt, because she was supporting him. When he slid down the side of the couch, however, he seemed to be quietly laughing. On the floor his head rolled. The boy lifted an arm, the left, and let it fall back and away from him, where the hand—like a spider, Greatman thought—felt and gripped the spindles of a dusty wooden chair.

"What is he saying?" Greatman asked.

"We don't know!" said the non-human girl.

"He needs help."

She clasped her hands, as if in delight. "Coffee?"

"Coffee?" he repeated.

But she seemed to have lost her place in the words they were speaking. "*Just—*" she said. "Wait."

At the stove, while he boiled water, he placed a conical wire filter in the mouth of a glass carafe. She admired his singularity.

Though Greatman enjoyed the sentiment, he couldn't trust it. Expressions moved the girl's face like weather, smooth and erratic. Nor did he trust the silence that had pushed in from the adjoining room.

The supine boy had interlaced his fingers over his chest. He refused coffee by closing his eyes and mouth.

Then—for the first time—the second boy spoke. "Just leave it, just set it down anywhere."

This boy wore boots. He'd lodged the sole of one to an edge of Greatman's coffee table. Leaning over his knee he studied the finds—locket, bead, dancer. Each had its own space. And each carried a function within something wider, a scheme whose principles, if veiled, were no less precise.

He had small eyes, with an excess of tissue, perhaps, in the lids.

He had crisp, flared ears. He wore black earrings.

Greatman held the coffee, about which he'd forgotten. He saw that it might be best if he cleared his face of any concern. In this he was too slow. The boy looked at him, looked to his eyes. He lifted the boot. He brought it down with dull force on the ceramic dog.

"Did you see that!" he cried, and he pointed at Greatman. "Did you see him?"

"What are you?—wait," said the girl.

"Watch."

Greatman didn't watch. The boot sole hammered the tabletop.

"That's just—" said the boy, taking in breaths. He kneaded his face—cheeks and eyes—as if to form an expression.

"Okay . . . okay . . . okay," said the girl.

"So the story," he said. "What's the story again?"

"Okay."

"There's a story. She's—factory-made?"

The boy's laughter was silent, nearly inert. Greatman saw that he bore the soul of a henchman. In time,

Greatman knew, someone was going to use this boy in the way that all such boys got used. He was scrap.

"You're scrap," Greatman tried to say, but he had to sit down.

Some of his finds had been ruined in the attack. The glass chess piece. The dog. The dancing girl. Most could be fixed or refurbished again. By daylight, however, the mess on the table and floor exposed a reality: here was nothing. Useless junk.

Greatman went walking.

Not having a reason or goal, he was different from those he passed, and he felt that this basic difference in him was perceived and at the same time ignored. He felt a consensus: that he should maneuver unseen, that unto him and him alone should be granted this final power.

But his thinking was off.

He stood in the street, in the rain, which found runnels in his skin, his bare chest. A woman came forward. The woman was limping, he thought. She held a coat. She said to him, "Please."

Because he could no longer bring himself to rise early, Greatman's habits collapsed. Sometimes he opted to keep to his bed, as if to see what would then happen. Of course, nothing did. His mind lulled. He followed the day by reading the light in his eyelids.

Someone knocked on his door. A neighbor. He didn't know which or why.

He showered, found food.

If he walked, he walked late. He sat on a bench in a

park that was small and not well-tended, and therefore not valued, and therefore empty, nearly always, when he was there.

He watched.

Pigeons.

Three people smoking some drug.

The winter sun as it made its descent through bands of speckled trees.

One time he saw someone on rollerblades, a person who resembled—and was, in fact—his acquaintance, the non-human girl.

Greatman had avoided the coffeehouse where they'd spoken, where she was employed. It hadn't been difficult. His appearance in that place could do nothing but pose accusation.

The skater—this person on rollerblades—wore wraparound sunglasses, black. She had dark, slanting eyebrows and matching tattoos of some kind on her wrists. She braked and turned back.

"I was thinking," Greatman said when she removed her glasses to declare herself. "Just now. May I tell you? Just before you came. I was thinking of a criminal. Of something he did. You may have heard of him. Alabaster, he went by."

The girl took a breath. "I wanted to say . . ." she began.

"A villain. A criminal of some repute. Sit with me?"

"Look," she said softly.

"Please."

From above came the sound of birds or squirrels moving around in dry branches. The rollerblade wheels were crimson and gold. They spun free once the girl sat down. Greatman breathed in. There was, on the crisp March air, a scent of firewood burning.

He said, "I'd been poisoned. This story—it's not very nice. Alabaster had poisoned me. Lethal gas. Then he buried me alive. Or he buried me half-dead. I had already started that journey. My death. Would you like to know how I knew?"

The girl tightened her frown.

"Because everything changed," Greatman told her. "Alabaster didn't matter. I didn't matter. Not in the way I might have thought."

She spoke with reluctance. "'Buried alive' . . ."

"In earth. I retched loam . . . But it wasn't like that. I've never told anyone what it was like. Not one of my chroniclers knows. I will tell you."

He waited.

The girl said, "Okay."

"Like a ball," he told her. "I rode a great ball, a clear ball, and the ball was spinning so fast I could see from all sides at the same time. I could see from the top, looking down at the vastness below, all the people, for whom I felt love. And I could see from the bottom, where I might have been nothing, where I was laid out—in magnificent weakness."

She cleared her throat. "What happened?"

Across the path and down from the bench, a host of sparrows rose. Greatman watched the birds as they zagged, pale breasts flashing in unison. "I was rescued," he said. "I'd forgotten that time. It's strange. I had completely forgotten."

"About what happened—at your place . . ." she started.

He turned.

"I'm sorry. I wanted to say that."

"You're good."

"I don't know," she told him. "But that's irrelevant, actually."

The girl stood on her wheels.

"If I may ask," he said. "What do those say?"

"What."

"Those." He pointed.

She turned out her wrists to expose the tattoos. It wasn't writing, Greatman realized now. It was thorn and vine.

That night, he lowered the panel in the hutch of the secretary and lit a candle. He intended to write to the non-human girl. A short letter. He wanted to say that he had enjoyed their talk on the bench and that he hoped he had not been too garrulous. But he couldn't begin. His pen left one mark on the sheet—the line of the 'D' in 'Dear.' This mark looked surprisingly actual; he sensed presumption, widening folly.

Greatman gazed at the shape described by the paper in wavering light.

For a time he did nothing. Eventually he stood up.

In the following days, he busied himself with tasks of immediate benefit. He swept floors. He removed two burners, scoured the pans beneath. He didn't often think of the non-human girl.

But he didn't avoid thinking of her.

In fact, he'd achieved a coherence on this subject, as he realized one night. He was out walking. The coarse black powerlines drooped webs in a luminous sky.

It couldn't have been for no reason, he saw, that he had been given her secret. It couldn't have been for no reason that he had been chosen. He alone heard.

The strange tale: a person born full-grown. Born fighting.

Greatman could do something here.

And he would. He couldn't say when, but he was prepared: he would give his protection, his light. In time, in his presence, she might come to feel that she could be soft in the way of most life, that she could be weak, like a child.

KISS OF THE UNDER-ACHIEVER

Twice I went into that bar, I think—unless I've conflated two different bars, alike in being singular, and in having no definite place on the map of the city I've made in my head.

The first time:

I was twenty. My eldest brother, Corey William, drove my car, which was, as he claimed—I made no argument—a total piece of shit. He was after a loser, a person who owed him cash (the sum he wouldn't divulge). He felt bad for this loser, whose rank on the loser scale would rise once everyone heard about the coming extraction of debt.

All right, said Corey William as he slowed to pull into the lot.

I'm remembering winter: the wiper blades scratching arches of granule over the glass; and how these arches seethed with offerings of light from cars when they passed.

I answered, All right.

Why don't you wait here? went my brother.

I knew that I'd sounded less than poised. Still, I

squinched up my eyes in offense.

Then we went in. Then all was transference. From darkness, amber spirit light. From cold, about two dozen freaks having some sort of battle with whipped-cream pies.

What can I do—what words can I use to make this sound more likely?

My brother ducked to the bar itself and got hit, I believe, in the shoulder. I stood by the wall. The people behind the bar—bartenders?—popped up to launch pies. There were pies on the tables, and others winging them. All this to the amplified sawings of '90s recordings of electric guitars.

I remember one person. His face was broad and red and circumscribed with sparse hair. He shook his head furiously. I mean that his head was a blur. He lashed his tongue from side to side, scooping in portions of cream.

I don't remember, with clarity, much else—which seems strange, given that history of some kind was being made here.

If I could venture a thought: we had, Corey William and I, taken a step beyond what could be supported in a normal way.

It was as if it hadn't happened. I mean later—afterward. It was as if we hadn't been there.

The next time:

I was older. Thirty, thirty-two. I went with this young kid, Tondy, who'd been part of a crew I'd been part of, that spring. A dock crew. We'd worked to install docks.

Tondy was slim. Facets of bone in his shoulders glowed in the petroleum steam of the convenience-store lot, which is where he and I had crossed paths. He was happy to see me. He began talking, right away, as if I was versed in his latest concerns, as if we'd been friends all our lives.

I thought there was something wrong with him, sort of. I thought he was light-giving, charmed.

He wasn't a cokehead. He didn't have, anyway, a cokehead's tense, businesslike mien. But he was after cocaine, which he said could be bought after-hours at a certain tavern he knew.

Off some freeway? Close to an underpass?

Weakish silver area light exposed a run of Junebugs, which moved in squirming unity, like parts of somebody's face. I said, Look at that. But Tondy had left me behind, already pushed through the doorway.

This time things were much slower—and more pure, I want to say. An old man with a lovely, beaten face talked about after the war. An unfiltered cigarette burned in his hand, which lay open, as if misplaced.

I stood near the ribboning float of that smoke. I tried to breathe its flavor.

From a barkeep, my former crewmate bought the drug in a little rectangular fold of glossy magazine page, then sat to prepare it—which he did in a modest way, keeping his backbone erect. From a girl at the bar, I bought a red ale. Her forearms were naked and dusked with black hair. Her eyes were a kind of see-through blue and caused my heart to panic.

But just for a second.

We were talking—she and I and others—about the past.

I was a shuffleboard champion, said one guy. I won a tournament that was held on the deck of a ship.

I was on TV, a woman's voice came. When I was ten. I sang a madrigal, a cappella. In Latin I sang.

The blue-eyed bartender drew a light beer. I was gifted—I was in gifted class, she said as the woman across from her, the singer, tried to locate the sounds of her song in a ruptured voice.

I closed my eyes, nodded my head, and held up my hand to be counted.

Later I kissed her. We stood in the frame of the hallway leading to the men's and ladies' rooms. The kiss wasn't heavy or too high-stakes. It had come, I'd have said, in a natural way, just part of the conversation: a kiss that was really a thought of itself, if thought was a factor at all.

What I mean: it was good. It bore no policy.

Isn't that grace? All foresight taken from you. You're nothing, just sticks of chance.

I thought I was there. I thought that I stood in that place.

But her lips released then—the bartender's. And though I didn't look up right away, I could see how things would be.

We stood in a hallway. We stood near restrooms, in a scent of disinfectant. In the jukebox, the stylus took the final groove of an Otis Redding song. A man stood, and in standing scraped the wooden floor with a leg of his chair.

He was apparently leaving. They were apparently closing, at last. The bartender's eyes were open but they had gone still, with the rest of her.

Tondy wondered what happened.

I said, What.

With the bar girl, he said as we coasted the 4 A.M. streets.

I pasted white drug to my fingertip and worked this into my gums.

That's cool if you don't want to talk about it.

No, I tried to explain.

That's cool.

Nothing happened.

Into the unmarked darkness ahead, for miles, the hanging traffic lights blinked red, like error messages. He asked, in a fraudulently casual way, where he was dropping me off. I told him I'd been there.

What?

That place, I said. I've been there before, I told him.

I KNEW GABLE ROY HENRY

In the late fall of 1946, I was a fifth-grade student under Miss Alison Leith at Adams Grade School, eight blocks through dry leaves or through snow from my home. Our state had just turned a hundred years old, as no child could possibly have failed to understand from the parades of the summer just past—or from the subsequent socials, which I still and will always recall for having lasted so wondrously late, past dusk, to that time when laughter was fugitive, to when lightning bugs shone in the corn rows beyond the dirt path that edged Elks Park. My father would have been thirty-one that year. He was working long hours to rebuild his practice, having served two years as a radioman overseas. Miss Leith and her colleague at the time I'll now speak of, Reed Manfred, would have been slightly younger, mid-twenties I would say. And Gable Roy Henry, though the name meant little, even if I had heard his songs—and we all had—would have been still a boy really, just twenty-three.

Miss Leith had accompanied our class in the move up from fourth grade. So we knew her already that fall, and she us. I'd go so far as to say that there was in our relationship a quality found in the best of homes, where fathers dipped their cheeks for quick goodbyes that smelled of aftershave, where mothers troubled coat buttons into stiff eyelets. Miss Leith was like that with us. Not affectionate—that's not what I mean to suggest—but brisk and familiar in the way of a parent. Absorbed. Implicitly allied. If someone caused trouble—if I, for instance, endeavored to impress some quiet young lady by feigning an episode of choking—Miss Leith did not blink and turn color, as would have been the case with Mr. Manfred; she simply announced that Tom Boyner would be spending some time in contemplation of the unadorned, tan-painted wall between the doors to the cloakroom. And as she led me back there, her hand at my shoulder, I received no sense that I was disliked or resented; she was merely impatient, perhaps—anxious to return to her lesson. That's how Miss Leith's fifth-grade classroom worked. Its mood was productive, steady, sure. It was like a fabric, heavily closing round us the moment we stepped through her door. No one fought it. The opposite, in fact. Many girls, and some boys (I include myself here), were loathe to spend time in the schoolyard, where a colder, chancier order held. And all of us, I think, felt a kind of alarm on the day when Mr. Manfred's helper appeared and Miss Leith failed to act as we knew her.

Mr. Manfred taught music and was new that year. He had replaced the corpulent Mrs. Devann, whose alert, managerial expression during 'Creative Time' (her own coinage) was broadly understood to be fraudulent and was mimicked on this account. Music at Adams was taught in the Audio-Visual Room, downstairs. This room housed wooden tables and chairs, a projector, and shelves replete with devices from which we could wrest distinct tones: wood ball mallets and sets of bells, autoharps, recorders, tambourines, sticks, an old phonograph with a detachable trumpet (off-limits), and a dimpled tin keypad that gave off a buzz at the touch of a thing that put me in mind of an eyedropper (deeply coveted). These were the means of Creative Time. If I can't understand how Mrs. Devann could endure it, I will say this: we students enjoyed it. I have one memory: hunkering down on the points of my knees and proceeding with strange devotion to work my thumbnail into the clay-red floor, which was made of a squishy material I've never seen anywhere since. Near the teacher's oak desk, beneath the loosely purposeful din of knocks and dings and whistles, I pressed in my name, working fast so that I might complete the "Boyner" before "Thomas" had faded. I have another memory. This one from the beginning of fifth grade. We enter the Audio-Visual Room, with its two big schoolhouse lights chained up like freighters sailing in place, and its musical toys, and we find not Mrs. Devann but another—a slender, beautiful man whose blond bangs have been trained to shadow one eye, wherein there appears harsh intelligence. This was Mr. Reed Manfred. In the short time he was to have at our school, he would make himself one of its most effective teachers, and perhaps its least liked. Creative Time was gone; and there would be no compensation—not in the way of sport, at least—

until the eventual arrival in that room of Mr. Manfred's
helper.

In the scratched scrap of film which I, like many
Americans, recently had the pleasure of seeing as part of
the Public Broadcasting System documentary, *Country*,
Gable Roy Henry is a skinny fourteen. I had questions
about this footage. For example, where did the camera
(antique even then, judging by the zip of its image) come
from? By what paths did it arrive at the Henry place,
twelve acres in Dry Ridge, Kentucky? The makers of
Country of course don't say. We simply see a shirtless
boy astride a thin motorbike. He notes the camera and
glances away, grinning at someone beyond the frame,
then looks back, his expression again speculative, closed.
Here the focus whips back from his face. The narrow rear
wheel of the bike spins cockeyed beneath him for maybe
a second or two before it and the bike and the loose-
shouldered boy take flight, or so it appears.

There's a moment when the picture falters and
clouds. There's another, right after, as it finds him again
(he's quite close now, fewer than ten yards away), when
Gable Roy Henry bears left and the wheels lose purchase,
beginning to slide. As I've said, the film's motion is fast:
and so, quickly—within the same instant, it seems—he
loses his grip, the bike hits down, and the bike rebounds
from widening dust straight into his waiting hands. It's a
magical image, as the filmmakers must understand, for
they choose to still the picture here, at the frame where
the bike has just risen from dust, where the eyes of the
very young Gable Roy Henry lift to the eye of the camera.

Seeing such footage, I wonder about fate. How is it that an image is recorded and preserved years in advance of the life and legend it will come to signify? Are the great somehow marked out from birth, held separate from us in a light that, while easily seen, must go for a time unsolved? Or is that just the fancy of hindsight? Is that just our way of dodging the prick of our failure to do something great ourselves? And do we not, thus indulging, deprive ourselves of the truth about figures like Gable Roy Henry—that they are people much like us, prone to unguessable melancholy at the cry of some bird in the hour of dusk, subject to pipe-dream crushes?

Vera may tease me all she likes for waxing on the subject of Gable Roy Henry. No matter. My questions stand.

It occurs to me for the first time after all these years—because questions never asked are never answered, I suppose—that the reason for Mr. Manfred's arranging for the help of the slender man whom we would call 'Tee' was that he—Mr. Manfred—could not play piano and direct us, or not both at the same time. And our town would probably not have considered budgeting a formal accompaniest. Reed Manfred's position itself was enough of a stretch for the men on our school board—men like Alison Leith's father, Eldon, and my own father, after whom I'd been named.

The piano in the Audio-Visual Room was an upright model the custodial staff had whitewashed at some point in time. Reed Manfred can't have approved of it, but indignation wasn't behind his reluctance to sit at the keys. He played standing because he had to; he wouldn't have been able to see us otherwise. And while his predecessor, Mrs. Devann, may have been happy to hide at the keys and run through sing-alongs, Mr. Manfred had higher purposes. He was going to take us students in the upper grades, who the year before had drooled into whistles and idly vandalized drums, and build an actual choir. He was going to direct us. I had no idea what that meant, at least in the early part of that year, so I couldn't appreciate how frustrating it was for him to have both hands tied up with the keys; in fact, I was thankful for the upright piano. It kept us from the man whose shoulders plunged, whose eyes, with slash-like wrinkles beneath, flashed our ranks so importunately. And when abruptly he stood and strode from the keys with his forearm bucking and drifting in time with the score, which of course was inaudible then, I'd stiffen. I sat at the front of the room (we'd been divided: boys in the alto section; across the aisle the sopranos, all girls). Mr. Manfred would range within inches of us, stopping at times directly above my chair, alive, impassioned.

"*Yes*," I remember him fairly shouting. Or "*No*," humming, flipping his bangs from his eye (there were atoms of sweat). Darting sideways, away from me. "*No*," humming it still, swinging his arms in wide alternation as if he could bodily gather our sound. And now "*Better*." Crouching, sensitively. Eyes nearly closed against what he heard. Lips small, and one hand—I'll never forget this— held in a miniature outward claw against the opposite cheek. "*That's it*."

We children—how did we take such behavior? Babe

Hancock, a rough, delirious boy whose faction I generally avoided, was moved to laugh outright. It happened early that fall. Mr. Manfred was, in his demonstrative way, beginning to work on a progression with the girls. We boys looked on in silence. Babe Hancock leaned forward and craned back around to see others and share his own baffled delight. When his mouth came open, a sound poured out that was high and light and dumb, and above all winning, so even those of us with sense enough to see what would happen couldn't help but join in.

He was taken by his shoulders, Babe Hancock was. He was shaken (Mr. Manfred's own arms shook). He was hissed at. We had to imagine the words, and that was of course much worse.

Thereafter we rarely crossed Mr. Manfred, or did anything that would have come naturally to us. There was a girl—April something. She had the gravest of young faces. When she had a cold, her mother would pin hankies to the chests of her dresses; April endured it. Mr. Manfred was leading the girls through a harmony they'd practiced and were supposed to have learned. He was miffed and pretending not to be, though not in a way meant to fool anyone, and the girls sang softly, wary of him, unwilling to offer him incontestable proof that they had forgotten. *I can't hear you, Robyn Gross.* He smiled, falsely. *I can't hear you, Diane Sage.* And they sang; they tried. *I can't hear you, April something. I can't hear you at all. Are you singing?* I can't tell you if April's voice was weak by nature, but she was quiet in a way that made even a boy of my shyness feel bad for her, and at the same time lucky—not to have been given what this girl had, not to have been put in an Earthly life whose deficiencies infected the very tones of her name, *April*, to the point where, years later, I couldn't have given a child that name, had we had one.

I can't hear you.

Alone, at a whisper, she sang.

I can't hear you. I can't hear you at all.

Her voice tried. There was nothing like music in it.

Are you singing?

April stopped, her small chin aquiver. One tear sped her cheek and vanished in the front of her dress, near the hanky. Another.

Mr. Manfred closed his mouth, glancing sharply about. I believe he would have welcomed then such conduct as you might expect of a class of fifth-graders— whispers and snickers and such, suppressions of nasty glee. He didn't get that. He looked from face to face, and in each met with icy compliance.

It couldn't have been long after that sad scene that Mr. Manfred brought in his new helper.

Let me say right now that I'm no expert on the life of Gable Roy Henry. Perhaps I know more than the next man about his ascent—to the Grand Ole Opry and beyond, to American superstardom, before he was out of his teens. And perhaps I have thrilled more often than most at his music, so haunting and simple, and looked more carefully at certain publicity shots: Gable Roy at nineteen, in glossy soft-focus, with tipped-back Stetson, crooked smile, ageless, deadpan eyes. But I won't pretend to be an authority. I'm unversed in the whispers following him from the curtained booth of the Memphis bar where he was so famously shot and killed by the dry-goods clerk—deaf, I believe—in 1951. In fact, I'm not interested—not enough, anyway, to have finished the Roland Sayer biography. In our town, independent of the life and legend, free of the attendant conjecture, there is a memory: that of a quiet young man who touched lives. This is all I concern myself with.

I understand that Mr. Sayer and others like him may well have a professional interest in the simple story I here record, since they, by consensus, have argued that Gable Roy Henry was likely in North Africa following the time of his service in the war—the 'missing' period. To them I say this: I aim not to light controversy; my purpose is neither scholarly nor tabloid. Should you have a desire to take my story further, you might begin by researching Reed Manfred, who left the county at the end of 1946, midway through the school year. He knew the man best. Myself, I wish only to set forth the memory of a town— its dimming encounter with a stranger of whom it still speaks with a marvelment that some might take for nonchalance, simply stating, "That was Gable Roy Henry."

The man was quite tall, or perhaps just appeared so to me on account of his huddled yet loose-going stride, silk-lined pant legs fluttering over bright boots. He was carrying a coat, I remember. The coat resembled a blanket, being made of plaid wool, and he held it folded in the cross of his arms as he walked the center aisle of the Audio-Visual Room. At the front, Mr. Manfred took him by the elbow, using just thumb and forefinger, and turned him around. The man's hair had been shaved, we could see. It tinted his scalp a pale, mouse brown. A faint redness seeped into his eyes from the inside corners. His mouth remained closed.

"Class, I would like to present Tee, my new helper. Tee, I would like to present our fifth-graders, the great hope of the Adams Grade School Concert Chorus."

The man's chin dropped in and then raised more slowly—a nod. And he looked at Mr. Manfred and blinked, and Mr. Manfred put fingers to the small of his back, then removed them and left them to hover there as he led him around to the upright piano, its bench. And Tee sat, disappearing. I listened to the wood swing back from the keys and to the yawn of the pedals beneath. I heard the first chord, midrange. It faded. There was little to be deduced.

That day, and for more than a week afterward, Tee did not speak. But he somehow wasn't a man who could do that. The lady who took pennies for milk, the men who scraped gray-headed mops through resonant hallways—these people could relax within themselves and did, and their faces were just faces, like walls are just walls; their faces did not open into our minds, marking them as people worth knowing about. They were simply grown-ups, with grown-up spaces to fill. And of course we were children: we ran about the legs of the milk-penny lady, hued legs, stockinged legs with their listless hiss, and we pressed through the door to the schoolyard and let it swing closed against the light.

But Tee was different. Even the dullest among us

could tell. When he entered, we oftentimes stared at him, and when he vanished behind the upright piano, our sense of his presence in the room did not weaken. We had only to witness Mr. Manfred's behavior—smoother, more amiable now, as if he liked us, as if he related to us—to recall that the new man, the helper, was seated back there at the keys.

"Thanks, guys," Mr. Manfred said once, that first week. We had just been freed to return to Miss Leith; students were leaving the room. "Really. You're all doing swell. I'm proud. You go home and tell your folks that. Tell them the voices of fallen angels have absolutely nothing on yours." He grinned down on us. I remember looking at him, then looking at the back of the piano, in whose crossbeams—angled, unfinished—the meaning of the force of the presence behind seemed intricately encrypted.

A Friday, then. His second at our school. There was a song. It had two slow verses and prior to the third an interlude of piano, and we were working on this—on our entrances, sopranos first, then altos: and it was all more complicated and subtle than kids our age should have had to contend with, perhaps. But we were trying. We were working, getting it wrong; and each time, Mr. Manfred asked Tee to go back and allow us to hear the interlude, which was pretty, and which hung from a single high note before falling to the point of our entrance. But the piano, alone, was so beautiful as to seem forbidding, at least to me. The piano was like a peaceable nursery, with kindred infants asleep, and our voices the graceless footsteps waking always a different one first. We could not get it right. Mr. Manfred, less nice by the minute, was sweating, snipping off time with his arm, flipping his bangs from his eyes. We listened, waiting. When the high note stretched and fell for what was to be the penultimate time, the sopranos trembled and wavered, yet ultimately held; we altos slurred it.

"No!"

He'd lost patience. Once more we waited for the piano. Once more we saw him march the floor and draw tight as the high note chimed and held, suspending itself over our failure. The high note stretched. One soprano peeped in early, dragging in two other girls. Mr. Manfred's eyes closed. As we waited, the high note fell, but not to the chord we knew; it fell to a naughtily prancing thing on low keys, a music played in matinees after some unfortunate creature got smashed by a falling anvil.

I believe we were all shocked. Mr. Manfred, his head at an odd, careful tilt, turned slowly to regard the piano, which had stopped playing. "I'm sorry?" Mr. Manfred said. And Tee rose, placed his elbows on top of the wood, let his chin come down in the x that was made by his hands and the cuffs of his shirt. One word he said: "Pardon." Their eyes negotiated then, Tee's eyes and Mr. Manfred's, and I'm not now able to tell you what, but something in the air between them freed us to beam, to stir, begin tittering.

"That was funny," I waited to say to him later, as he passed.

"Bye, Tee," said Janie Puhl.

And the following week—when he walked in late,

smelling of smoke and outdoor cold, plaid jacket folded and draped to his arm like a blanket: "Hi, Tee."

"Hello, Tee."

And Janie Puhl: "My goodness but that's a handsome shirt, Tee."

It was brazen to address a teacher like that, if not scandalous. But Tee was not a real teacher, and Mr. Manfred, it appeared, was less interested in Janie Puhl than in seeing what his helper meant to do.

Tee stopped, half-turned. "Thank you . . . Janie?"

Janie Puhl blushed with honor.

Two students then spoke from different parts of the room.

"Look, Tee!"

And: "What was that thing on the piano?"

Mr. Manfred said, "That's enough."

This was the week we stopped fearing him, though. This was the week, back upstairs, in our classroom, when whispers began to replace gloom upon the announcement that it was time for us to file down to Music. And this was the week when Miss Leith (who had noticed—who would have been curious about the change yet perhaps too well-bred to be seen prying) began making that announcement later each day, in seeming forgetfulness. The long hand would pass the top of the dial by three minutes. Four. Five.

"How silly of me," she may have planned on saying when Mr. Manfred had finally been drawn up the two flights of stairs.

I stress: this is only conjecture, though. And it was not, anyway, Mr. Manfred who came.

*

In the novels Vera has read to me during the drives which I've called—nostalgically, perhaps—our 'motoring tours,' I have trouble fashioning faces from words. Of course, this is not my problem right now. It is yours, and will be compounded by the fact that my sense of the features of Mrs. Walter P. Mack, née Alison Leith, has changed—not so much with advancing age, but according to my changing relationship to her. A year after I entered high school, she became vice principal. When I think of her face in those years—the slender, wide jawbones, hung almost like earrings of a sort she would never have worn; the straight lips—I can't really separate it from her uncanny way of appearing at just those times when it was least convenient for you to have to explain yourself: and cast in light of that memory, her face can't be termed attractive. Later, when we, like our fathers, both sat on the school board (our terms overlapped for two years), I knew her to be a woman of unforced confidence and ability. I was gratified to work with her, and I found her then a real pleasure to behold, character implicit in each of the lines in her face. And so she still is, may I say: in her nineties, a widow, a resident out at the care center, Alison Mack is yet a handsome woman.

And in 1946? When she was Miss Leith? When she was my fifth-grade teacher? I suppose I'd have said, if asked, and if pressed—because always I stalled coquettishly when grown-ups asked me questions—that Miss Leith was pretty. I suppose, too, that I would have been right. She was a young woman. She'd taken on duties to which she was suited. We liked her, needed her.

All of this Tee might have chanced to observe on that day when, sent to collect us, he paused at our door. All of this Tee might have gathered just hearing her voice, just watching her arm as it moved to the stroke of her hand on the chalkboard. I ask you: how could he not have been taken?

In that room, I sat toward the front, on the left—the last name 'Boyner' placing me behind Haley Ash and in front of the smartest one in the fifth grade, Judy Brooks. Past an aisle, low radiators piped a silvery note—like birds, I thought at the time, like fantastical birds who could fly undersea and from there, from deep down, were now calling. I envisioned pterodactyls. But I had to restrict my imaginings; I could not, for example, gratify the urge to look out the windows at the turnaround drive where some of us were picked up every day at 3:30, and two flags, our country's and state's, rolled on occasional breeze. I had to follow the lesson. And I didn't particularly mind. The radiators sang, Miss Leith's chalk tapped the board. These sounds, and a color of light—a pale yellow—enclosed me far more, it seems to me now, than the room's six physical planes.

I wasn't the first to notice him. I was bent to my desk, working on math, when I sensed a wave of movement among my classmates and turned to my right: he was standing there, Tee, in our doorway, one hand around back of the jamb. So anchored, he let the weight of his shoulders tip in, then pulled himself straight. Miss Leith turned.

"May I help you with something?"

Though the words were beyond fault, and though I knew both Tee and Miss Leith to be generally cordial, there was, right away, some species of trouble: it was as if all the air in the room was now subject to a draw of certain slow force.

Tee nodded, not in affirmative response but in greeting. "I'm helping Reed Manfred downstairs," he said, adding, "with the piano."

Miss Leith remained still.

"I'm Tee."

A bit of hushed mischief ensued. Miss Leith glanced at us. "I wasn't aware . . ." she began.

"I'm just helping. They've got a big program coming up here, these kids."

And again she said nothing. From where I sat, across the room from the door and in a direct line with it, I could not see her face. But I could see his. A shaved cowlick at the crown of his head held light like a piece of scratched metal.

As I recollect, Miss Leith introduced herself now, and Tee nodded and told her that it was a pleasure, continuing by way of conversation to ask what she did when we were in Music.

"Put your books away, please," she told us. To him she said, "Pardon?"

"When the kids are downstairs," he repeated. He went on, not pausing for response this time. I had some difficulty hearing him now, for students were shifting about in their seats, getting ready, and he'd lowered his voice. I leaned closer.

To the best of my knowledge, what he said had to do

with our objectives in the Audio-Visual Room. I heard him refer to a song we'd worked on, "Bellflower." He may have added that the lyrics were taken from Longfellow, thinking this fact might interest her, a school teacher. And he may have invited her down to watch. This I can't say. What is certain is that Miss Leith turned from him, even as he was speaking to her, even as he, in expression and gesture, appeared to be gaining enthusiasm. Miss Leith turned away, and I could see that she'd narrowed one eye. It was as if she was bidden to consider some matter more important than what he was relating.

I was a little confused.

Then again I was a ten-year-old child. What could I possibly hope to understand of the heart, its age-old reflexes?

Christmas at Adams was marked by the appearance of a small tree beside the desk of the school secretary, who was also named Adams. "Miss Adams of Adams," we all sang. The limbs of her tree were of soft green nylon. Its hue-coated bulbs could be seen through the office window from the turnaround drive on a dark winter morning: blue and ruby, they were, red-orange, dandelion yellow. In the office one time I touched one; I cannot tell you why. It was hot. I was reprimanded.

Christmas at Adams was marked by the coming of snow. Were there seasons without? I am old. They have vanished. Memory finds its scene in snowflakes falling clustered, as wide as buckeyes, to cover that crunchy half-circle of grass described by the road and the turnaround drive, and thereafter to cover themselves alone. Such snows made fancy revisions upon all things. Such snows persisted. With exposure to midday sun, they might soften, yield granular snowballs, perhaps. Then, overnight, they could freeze up completely, preserving the wild topography of our footprints, and presenting a hazard for Mr. Tillwarden, whose daily task it was to hoist up the pair of flags.

In our classroom, on the other side of the many-paned windows through which Mr. Tillwarden's steps were monitored (in hopes, I confess, of a spill), Christmas was marked by cut-paper snowflakes and chains, and in a truer, more stirring way by the cloakroom, a walk-in passage at the back of the room with doors on each side. In December, the cloakroom turned into a place of thick coats and long scarves, knit mittens, knit hats, rubber boots, and the little voiceless sighs of us children trying to get out of them. At lunch, if one thought to hide oneself here—and I seem to remember occasions—one would see that small puddles had formed on the floor. One would find that the human breath frozen in scarves had melted: tiny droplets stood on single kinks of wool.

In years previous, in the time of Mrs. Devann, the Three Kings might appear in our sheet music, journeying piously; if so, we could always rouse ourselves to switch verses and place the exploding rubber cigars to their solemn lips. That aside, the season brought no real change to proceedings in the Audio-Visual Room—not until the year the new teacher arrived; the year that Reed Manfred, assisted by the man whom we would know only as 'Tee,' gave us the Adams Grade School Christmas Program.

I can't with any certainty say when preparations began. When I think of Reed Manfred's time at our school, when I recall his peculiar intensity, I think automatically of the Program. It was his mission. I don't exaggerate here. The Christmas Program was what he saw to make his eyes flash at us so.

"Rise, Rise, Rejoice" was the name of the first song we practiced. Reed Manfred was probably concerned about the song's duration and the fact that it was to be performed by all three upper grades as the Program finale. But we were not told this. So for me—as for others, I suspect—"Rise, Rise, Rejoice" was something of a chore: too simple, it seemed; too harshly exultant; stuffed with too many *thous*. Better was a song whose real name I never learned; "Pasture of Whitest Snow," we called it. The song told the story of a quiet young girl who prevails upon her father to step off the path one night, to enter a clearing—there to witness an angel. *In a pasture of whitest snow.* I found this story quite beautiful. As for the song, our second time through, I was in love. I wanted to hear it again, right away. I cherished the too-brief melody of its refrain, and I envied the girls, whose part that was, nearly to the point of hostility.

Of another order entirely was the pleasure we took in the song we did with just Tee. I will detail this more thoroughly, as there are historical implications.

On a Monday in late November, with preparations for the Program already well underway, Tee came into

the Audio-Visual Room rubbing his hands. His arrival
proceeded ours by about ten minutes, as it did from time
to time—and without our thinking to chide him for not
being punctual. In this, we took our cue from Mr.
Manfred. When Tee came in that day, Mr. Manfred
didn't glance at his watch; he just smiled. Warmth
reconfigured his eyes. "Tee!" some said. Then, because
we felt we might never see enough of this man who
turned to the piano each day, we watched him: his
walking the soft red aisle, blowing on fingers of right and
left hand, rubbing the palms together to make a papery
kind of sound. And it might have been anytime. It might
have been any other day—Tee's arrival, its scent: the
smoke, the big cold—except this was the day Mr.
Manfred stepped into the aisle and blocked Tee's passage.

Between them there was a difference in height—five
inches, let us say. Mr. Manfred, the slighter, chose not to
cast threat as Tee stopped before him at the head of the
aisle, but rather a spritely, teasing kind of resistance. Tee
pardoned himself and moved left; Mr. Manfred was there
to receive him. Tee went right; Mr. Manfred performed a
little hop and cut him off. Both men at this point held
still for a time, Tee looking squarely down at Mr.
Manfred, and Mr. Manfred, through the soft blond fall of
his bangs, looking up. Behind him, he held his baton in
both hands, the tip of it touching his spine. It was as if
the baton was a gift of some kind. It was as if he intended
to give it to Tee, but only when Tee had quit guessing.

Tee squinted.

"You promised," Mr. Manfred said.

"What."

"You said." And he brought one hand around and pointed in the direction of the door. We children waited. Our silence pressed in on itself. So when Tee feigned a grab at the shorter man's ribs, at the soft place just underneath, and Mr. Manfred cried "Say!" in shrill and giggling surprise, we exploded. We howled, we squealed. Janie Puhl stretched her hands like stars, and they shook, they just trembled with pleasure. It took Mr. Manfred nearly as long to calm us as it took his helper to leave and come back, this time with a suitcase, long and black and misshapen, aside his leg.

I'd never seen a guitar. I'd seen the kiddie versions, fancifully painted *Wild West* and strung with something like fish line, but never a guitar. Imagine my feeling then when Tee, not three yards away from me, popped the gold clasps, flipped back the lid, and pulled his into the light. How solid an object! How precise, deliberate! Idly he rapped its strings with his thumb as he settled himself on the desk, and the report was so pure, so whole and deeply alive, that I felt in the moving blood of my hands a yearning to reproduce it. I wanted that guitar. I wanted to test its heft, feel its mirrory woods. Tee was twisting its polished chrome pegs, the tone in the chamber responding. I watched the frets wink. I watched the untrimmed string ends shiver. If somehow you could have spied my young face, surely you'd have seen in it a slack and unsightly longing, a look almost of pain.

Then he played. His hands configured a chord, and another, another again. I can't state beyond doubt that the song was "Come Springtime," for he left off too quickly, and without singing. It remains my personal belief, however, that it was. The song, from what little we heard, had the vibe of "Come Springtime," that prodigal lift. And certainly we couldn't have felt any worse when he stopped, when his hands quit making it.

"No!" someone called.

And outraged, "*Tee.*"

And it was then as it was so many times later, Tee bemused at the instant animal clamor he could incite, Mr. Manfred having to intervene, reestablish order.

For the record, I give you the title of the song we were taught that afternoon: "Christ's Born Today." I've offered the lyrics to an acquaintance of mine, a musicologist, formerly at Creighton. She has yet to get back to me. I've attempted my own research too; so far, though, I have found nothing. As a result, you will have to be satisfied with no more than what you, on your own, might deduce—that the song was a standard, or variant thereof, which I in my ignorance and lack of resource have not been able to identify; or that it was new, an original, performed just once, in a school in an Iowa town, and never recorded: a simple Christmas song, unique in its author's known work, for here he turns his God-given music toward God; he sings to His glory.

Shepherds lift your lonesome eyes . . .

It was a hymn. Its tempo was steady and slow, its melody plain and strong. And we all sang melody; there was to be no tinkering, no dividing of parts. In this sense, it was one of our easiest songs, and we might have dispatched it inside of a day if we had been following Mr. Manfred instead of Tee's voice—that marvel of strength and reach and candor which made us close up our mouths just to listen. Still, we learned quickly, so that by our second day of practice Tee's vocal was no longer needed, except for his two-word part—half spoken, half sung. I remember Miss Leith was downstairs on the day we mastered it. Mr. Manfred was keeping loose time with his baton while leaving the real direction to Tee, who in fact did nothing but sit on the desk and play while she watched and we sang.

> *Shepherds lift your lonesome eyes*
> *And cast your blues away*
> *Can you hear on these dark skies*

And Tee stopped playing: "Hear what?"

> *Christ's born today*

And with strength he started playing again, and I peeked at Miss Leith, knowing I'd find in her face every sign of approval.

She was also present for the tryout after school one day, but this will require some prefacing.

By any measure, things were going nicely downstairs in the Audio-Visual Room by early December. Reed Manfred, no doubt emboldened by the progress we'd made, announced that he was going to be holding auditions on an upcoming Wednesday afternoon for a special small-group piece that might—and he stressed that—*might* serve as an encore for our Program, to be sung after we and the fourth- and sixth-graders had bellowed out "Rise, Rise, Rejoice." Like my classmates, I received the news blankly, silence in this case having the advantage of not seeming inconsistent with either interest or indifference. And we had reasons to show both. I personally liked Mr. Manfred and hoped not to hurt his feelings by dismissing the prospect. Others may have feared offending him; I don't know. Certainly, though, no one—with the exception of Judy Brooks, who raised her hand and asked if it would be possible to see the music—was immediately willing to have it known that he was a student so enamored of school as to want more of it, on his own time, after the bell, especially since the teacher in this case was Mr. Manfred. We had long since made our peace with him, yes, and in truth we loved working with him and with Tee; at the same time, who among us did not recall his first month, when any show of tolerance toward him would have brought on playground ridicule, and not of the common sort, either—a ridicule likely infused with the whole trapped weight of resentment the man had inspired? So we were mostly silent. We declared nothing. I filed from the room, aware of some muted, inner point of concern that seemed related to the fact that Judy Brooks had asked to see the music and was presently seeing it.

In those weeks, after school had let out, at 3:30, I'd find myself wandering the pearly blue chill of abrupt evening, in the glow of wreathed lamps, to stand at the window of Busy B Shoes, a shop on Center Street. This walk took me several blocks out of my way, which can make a difference in an Iowa winter; there was, however, in the window of that store, a child-sized pair of Western boots made by Acme and marked—prohibitively, I feared—at ten dollars, ninety-five cents. They were black, like Tee's. They had double-stitched shapes up the sides. Long minutes I'd stand in contemplation of them, hands balled, empty mittens hanging from snot-glazed sleeves like frozen tongues, and by the time I finally turned back to the street, the cold would have crafted a sting at the exact center of my forehead, a buzz in my toes. At home then, on our well-shoveled stoop, I could not turn the knob or do anything but lean against the doorbell, whose chime, repeating, came as if from a music box. Then the door would rip back. And how lovely the scoldings were then! How soothing the force of my mother's two hands, undoing each button, each hard, frosted knot. I was inert, a piece of anything at all in the totality of warmth and light.

We ate dinner alone, my mother and I. She drank, which is another story in the truest sense: another memory, not part of the part of my life that I'm able to date. I will say, out of loyalty (and what loyalty is there like that of a son, grown old and solely responsible for the memory of a parent?)—I will say that she was no one's caricature: lugubrious at the rim of the glass, if you like; or quaking with counterfeit poise. She was no one's old story. Beyond that, I offer you only conclusions formed half my life ago now, and many years after the fact: that my father, in a way, had been more open and accessible in wartime letters than he was later, upon his return. The office had taken the place of the war, but without letters. He no longer counseled me as to the

relative merits of slider and curve ("We played baseball
on deck today, Tommy . . ."). And he did not write my
mother, in a tighter hand, those long paragraphs ending
'my love.'

Dinners with my mother were held in the close,
bright kitchen, as during the war. I recall that on the day
Reed Manfred announced auditions for the special small-
group piece she asked if there was something the matter,
to which I said no. It was not a lie, though I was capable
of telling one if I judged it would somehow satisfy her.
And it was not quite the truth; I felt mildly agitated, in
fact. The feeling would not speak its name.

"Nothing's the matter?"

"No."

And the radio cracked softly on its shelf, nearly
beneath hearing.

Of the next night I can tell nothing save that any
stirrings I felt at dinner were no longer their own secret;
they were mine. I had seen Judy Brooks conferring with a
friend outside Miss Leith's classroom. I had seen Jacob
Green, a favorite of Mr. Manfred's, examining something
in his notebook, which he found reason to close when I
passed by. And I could not be sure then. Mr. Manfred
reminded us for the last time about the audition, and
there was again silence, but this time I could not be sure.
Did they all, every one of my classmates, mean to be at
the audition Wednesday afternoon? Were they
determined, and was the apathy of their postures a ploy
to discourage turnout? I looked about the room. I looked
at Jacob Green, Robyn Gross, others. If they had their
secrets, though, I had mine. I cradled it fearfully there,

and at home with dreaming excitement.

Then on Wednesday I pretended to start home after school. But turned. Started back. Went down to the Audio-Visual Room in an agony of shame equal in intensity only to my later joy upon reading my name, *Thomas Boyner*, on the handwritten list tacked to the bulletin board.

That joy! Pushing out on the white of my breath as I stood at the window of Busy B Shoes. Making me shudder and bounce in my bed in the dark when I should have been sleeping.

Reed Manfred selected twelve students that afternoon. At the audition, contrary to what I had feared, there were only about twenty of us present—more from my class, Miss Leith's fifth grade, than any other, and not many representing the fourth. The procedure: Reed Manfred taught us a verse, then auditioned us in pairs, a soprano, an alto. More quickly than I would have believed, I was up, I was through. I stood and blinked at the next pair; by the time I thought to find my own partner, Judy Brooks, and go over what I could recall, she'd left. I tiptoed, looking for her. It was then that I noticed Miss Leith standing back at the wall and whispering something or other to Tee as they observed the two singers.

While 1942's "Come Springtime" is for me, as it's been for generations of Americans, not only an awesome testament to the simple grace that marks true perfection in art but also a friend and inspiration, I take pleasure in having a handful of more personal favorites among

Gable Roy Henry recordings, one of these being a song called "Unsigned Roses," which was released by Decca in the spring of '47, and which, according to my research, went as high as number eight on the country charts. The refrain is as follows:

> *Up round your stair-way*
> *Down your hall floor*
> *Can't see my way*
> *But I'm in through your door*
> *Your face in moon-light*
> *Lord what I'd do*
> *But you never knew*
> *Sleepin' one I loved*

I recall that upon first hearing the song I thought it strange that passion's object should be so disfigured—a 'sleeping one-eyed love.' But it was later, in the sixties, when George Jones did the song, that I developed my special attachment to it—and for reasons not having to do with George Jones but with certain ideas that began to unfold for me then, and that I would here offer. "Unsigned Roses," first of all, was but the second release after Gable Roy Henry's resurfacing, in 1947. No mention is made as to sources for the song in the Roland Sayer biography, and while I realize that any popular song will apply less to the particulars of the writer's life than it will to the norms of its genre, I would nonetheless stress the unusual situation we find in "Unsigned Roses": a love that is never disclosed and yet is not without intimacy; a gift of flowers, common enough, but delivered in trespass, touched to the pillow, extended directly into the heat of the mysterious loved one's breath. Is it too much to suggest that this was a picture that Gable Roy Henry knew something about? Am I going too far if I propose that in "Unsigned Roses" he undertook to describe a love that may be entered upon even when circumstance defies its unveiling? I'm thinking of course of Miss Leith. Of her and Tee at the white piano. I'm thinking of the stir of those innocent whispers that must have passed between them.

Judy Hente, née Brooks, who now lives in Council Bluffs and whom Vera and I still see occasionally, believes there might in fact have been an explicit relationship. She points to the fact that after school, during practice (for Judy too was one of the twelve), Miss Leith did not bother to greet or formally acknowledge Reed Manfred when coming downstairs but instead went directly to the piano, where she conversed with Tee during much of our practice. Remember, this was sixty-some years ago. That anyone recalls it as clearly as I is a thrill. She continues, Judy does: decorum would not have allowed one teacher to enter another's classroom so freely; only if there had been a relationship, understood by all three, would Miss Leith have thought to enter the room with such assurance. Furthermore, there was, as Judy recalls, some tension: it was as if Miss Leith enjoyed the possibility that her way of entering would be taken as rude, as if Mr. Manfred, in turn, enjoyed ignoring her. Such tensions, Judy reminds me, are characteristic of the jealously that sometimes develops between the new lover and the longtime friend.

I respond simply: these were innocent times. I very much value Judy's perspective on a memory so few of us share, yet I must counter: these were different, less cynical times—times when Miss Leith's quiet entrance might have signaled respect for the instruction in progress; times (to use Judy's own example) when a child, realizing that she would be late for school, and distressed as a result, could accept a ride from an acquaintance of her uncle. Innocent times. Young people could nurture the bittersweet pleasures of an impossible crush in such times, and without going further. Celebrities could vanish, blend back in, be taken for simple strangers.

At least for a time. Something happened the night of the Program, something the former Alison Leith alone has certain knowledge of, but which I, more than anyone else perhaps, am qualified to speculate on.

The song we twelve had won the right to perform was a madrigal. I came to enjoy the sound of that word, as I came to enjoy the sound of the words inside it— *sanctorum*, I particularly recall—once I recovered from finding that the song had lyrics (we'd *la*'ed it in audition) and that the lyrics it had were not part of the English language. And that wasn't the only issue. Mr. Manfred had adapted the song from four parts but had sacrificed few of its showcase features—the triplets, the half-note rests. As a result, it gave us twice the trouble of "Pasture of Whitest Snow," and we had had weeks to master that one. Here, we had just seven days. Five practices. Four, not counting dress rehearsal. Worse, Mr. Manfred insisted that the song be performed—*if at all,* was his ongoing threat—a capella. We regarded him like dogs when he first told us, waiting for him to see folly. But he never did. And so, with just a hook of his baton, he forced us out of the silence. But the topper was yet to come. Tuesday, on the eve of the dress rehearsal, Mr. Manfred led the way to the auditorium and asked us to sing the song hand in hand. I prayed it was an instructional device; it was not. He arranged us by height and part (I stood between Jacob Green and a sixth-grade boy whose name now escapes me, an erect, confident, dark-haired boy with a certain striped shirt—plum and cream—that I still recall helplessly admiring). Then he made us hold hands: palm to palm, flesh to flesh; warm or cool, chalky or smooth, callused or soft or perspiring. And if we failed to wrap fingers—if any two of us did—it made the awkward details of such contact come all the more keenly alive.

I'd imagined I might have more access to Tee as one of the chosen twelve. He did stand close to me one afternoon, boots shining, wool jacket redolent of smoke, and say, and I quote, "How you doing there, Thomas?" And of course I was speechless with thrill. But whatever rarefied world I'd imagined in the days leading up to the audition, it didn't materialize. There was no sense of being taken inside Tee's circle; only of working in obscure coordination with various half-glimpsed others. We heard hammering, sawing. Other teachers would appear. Such an atmosphere did have an appeal of its own, but we twelve were not free to absorb it—or absorb anything beyond the sounds of the song and the sleepless gaze of our director. If I regret anything at all, it is that: the fact that we, in our push to prepare, did not have the chance to appreciate the time as we should have, to blink and look about, hang each detail in our minds. Hindsight deepens and turns this regret. The picture: I enter school for the first time after Christmas, in the new year. I walk down halls unchanged despite all seeming, despite the wondrous report of my bright black Acme cowboy boots, which I'm eager to wear in Tee's presence and have him see: I clop downstairs. I make for the Audio-Visual Room, whose door, I see, is ajar, and I enter, look up. And feel my heart now. Feel the heart of a ten-year-old boy as he sees that someone, without thinking it necessary to tell him, has removed Mr. Manfred, removed Tee, replacing them with this other man. Spectacles. Jowls.

"Yes?"

Feel my heart.

In later years, I would understand, of course; all told, it was no great mystery. There were men in attendance the night of the Program, men like my father and Eldon Leith, to whom the unsanctioned presence among the children of a man who wasn't known, a stranger who had supplied not even his last name, was cause for action. I have a surreal memory of my father, my busy father, taking me aside, into his study, seating me near the medallion of light on his desktop, asking me questions. I believe now that my father—and I confess I'm the same—experienced a thrill he found hard to suppress at being in any way touched by events of potentially grave import. He questioned me closely, face lit with seriousness, and within such sudden and total focus I floundered, did not know my name. He voiced questions. *Did he speak to you? What did he say? Did he touch you?* I gazed past the light on the desk at my father, bewildered, agog.

A collection of twenties' Westerns has passed through my family, from my grandfather to my father, from him to me. Cloth covered in faded oranges and greens, they're of a height. Any one can be taken in hand, gripped by its thickness of spine. And that moment is best, before the first opening, when each volume is equally charged with its secrets, each one holding a potency not ideal—not derived from thought—but true, concrete: the sensation of a stone in one's palm before throwing. That is what I mean.

Why offer such contemplation? Because the time has come, the time to crack the spine of the last volume. And while I do so gladly, I'm nevertheless aware of our passage into the part of the account where what happened is what happened, where it's my job to deliver 'the goods' and yours to feel how you will. The stone is let go. Perhaps I have given this too much buildup. Perhaps the material itself is too thin—one hour, some sixty years back . . .

But the time has come.

Dress rehearsal, I must first say, was on a Wednesday, a week after the audition. It was not a dress rehearsal at all in the sense you're probably familiar with, but rather a walk-through, with special attention paid to the artful entrance and exit patterns Mr. Manfred had

devised. I won't dally here. You can certainly imagine for
yourselves the pleasantly stimulating confusion of the
scene in the auditorium. You will understand that we,
the wide-eyed students of five classes, couldn't be
depended upon to attend Mr. Manfred unless he was
right in our faces, and that, as a result, several teachers
had to be there, enjoining us to move or keep still as the
situation required.

One thing: Miss Leith was not present. Not that it
made a great difference; other teachers were there. I'm
certain I would have forgotten her absence completely
had she not, toward the end of the rehearsal, made her
entrance, and 'entrance' is truly the word: the sight of her
was a match for the lit stars on the backdrop Mr.
Tillwarden had erected on stage, or for the marvelous
feedback issuing now and then from the microphone.
Had she come from some gala? Was she just then en
route? I am able to say only this: that Miss Leith had
arrived in an evening dress—off-white, and spectacularly
fitted. Her shoulders were bare. Understand, we're
talking about a smallish town, and at a time when
fashions for women had yet to shirk wartime austerity.
Alison Leith was a vision. Judy Hente supplies further
detail: that her hair had been looped and pinned to her
head like some exotic shell; that her throat, beneath the
wide jawline, was banded by a doubled choker of pearls;
that she held up the front of her dress in both hands as
she made her way down between the fourth-graders
seated cross-legged in the aisle. *A picture-book princess*,
says Judy with a knowing grin. And what harm is there in
agreeing with her? What harm in conceding the

insinuation—that Miss Leith entered the auditorium that day with such a splash as could hardly have been guileless, she whose presence was not needed, would not have been missed?

So she wanted to be seen. So she carried a hope: that amidst the general admiration, a particular man's feeling might grow.

I find no fault here.

The next night, Thursday, the nineteenth of December, 1946, it was my mother's turn to dress before the mirror, which image now teases me with the forgotten scent of her perfume. It was a mild night, the air exacting no toll on the cheeks for a look at the moon. And there issues this memory: walking in front of my parents as we came within sight of the school, and thinking how sharp, how fabulously remade it appeared, tall windows lit against the night.

Inside I had to separate from my parents, of course—which I didn't mind; I considered it unfair, nonetheless, that they were shown in through the big double doors to the auditorium, while I, whose Program it was, had to line up in the hallway. But I have to say I was luckier than most. With Miss Leith, I stood at the front of the line of fifth-graders and so just to the left of the doors. A fourth-grade girl stood opposite me, to the right, and behind her the rest of her class, and behind them the unlucky sixth-graders, who probably couldn't hear much of the Program's first highlight—the third-graders singing behind Tee. At the first tunings, Tee's fingers and thumb in the strings (as caught by a standing microphone), I leaned forward but felt Miss Leith's hand at my arm. So I just listened: there was guitar (Tee had begun), and wooden blocks played by some lucky third-grader, suggesting the clop of reindeer. *Up on the house top*, the third-graders sang. And now only the sound of wood blocks could be heard. *Down through the chimney with old Saint Nick.*

Afterward the double doors were pushed in: second- and third-graders streamed past us in tandem, looking radiant, dazed. It was our turn. Behind me students pressed forward, eager to get their first glimpse of the space and the crowd, whose applause was enormous. Miss Leith was inside now, holding the door. I crept forward; I could not resist. The auditorium was dark except for the lights on the aisles and those coming from the center of the stage, from a contraption Mr. Manfred had dubbed, rather whimsically, the 'Fruit Machine.' Standing beneath the blue backdrop, which had been strewn with tin-foil stars, this device consisted of an ice cream tub that spun on a tiny slow motor. Inside was a floodlight. Colored transparencies overlay cuts in the upended bottom: a display of what looked like the northern lights bled into the picture of night. To my eyes, it was extraordinary. I kept glancing away at Miss Leith, expecting at any moment to find I had drawn her admonishing stare. But my teacher was preoccupied: on tiptoes, she peered left and right. Mr. Manfred was gone—backstage, I supposed—and Tee too. The applause had begun to die out, and there was to be heard, in conjunction with the Fruit Machine's visuals, a lively flute concerto coming from the school phonograph. We were in the First Interlude. For several minutes, according to Reed Manfred's plan, music and light were to play, intertwine, while suspense for the performance of the upper-grade students built slowly among members of the audience. I looked for my parents. All heads were in darkness. Miss Leith turned around, and I got back in place but too slowly. As I recall, her reprimand came in the form of a catlike hiss.

Our own entrance was designed to overwhelm. The fourth-graders stepped down the center aisle at a ceremonial pace. I waited for the last to pass through. With the first sixth-grader, I then led a double line of students into the darkness, not looking at the grown-ups who turned in their seats, and not taking the steps to the stage as the fourth-graders had but rather splitting to the left to lead my class to one side, where we were to wait. This was not overly difficult. Responsibility nonetheless fell on me as one of the leaders in line, and I cherished it, hummed with the charge of it, and in this way failed to hook into the fourth-graders' performance. Next it was us. I had been at the front of the line for our entrance; I was last for our climb to the stage, the final student to take his place in front of the risers. And just as I did, I saw Tee, who'd moved away from the piano. He was dressed unexpectedly—in a Western-styled suit, light tan, with brown embroidery, and a matching tan hat. He was dressed, that's to say, like who he was. And as captivating as Alison Leith had been in her gown the night before, Tee was even more so, for the simple reason that he didn't behave as if 'dressed up,' that no sense of fine difference came over him now as he sat and lowered the brim of his hat to fit through the strap of his guitar.

And now he started. We started. I was actually clear-headed just then, as it became real.

Shepherds lift your lonesome eyes . . .

You will say that it is distance, the awareness of history's touch, which leads me to select this song, this moment, as my personal highlight of the Christmas Program, and perhaps there's truth in that. And yet, though "Pasture of Whitest Snow" was moving, a song offered softly, with feeling, and though "Rise, Rise, Rejoice," the finale, was a knockout, delivered by us and the fourth- and sixth-graders as if to oppose some assault, the song we performed with Tee was in a way the most memorable, for the song with Tee was the one that changed most between schoolroom and stage. In the Audio-Visual Room, the song had been fun. Here, it broadened. It hatched. Moved free. White light blanked my vision, but I was certain that the grown-ups in the audience were enthralled by the living work of the song. I was certain they felt what I felt and, like me, were astonished to find themselves feeling it.

I have not mentioned Mr. Manfred. That should come as no surprise; a director's work, even more than that of a coach, is done in advance. After "Rise, Rise, Rejoice," amidst pounding applause, Mr. Manfred extended a sweeping arm toward us, the combined upper-grade students, and then toward the piano, where Tee could be seen to stand. In my memory, the applause here burgeons. In my memory, Mr. Manfred, bangs sweaty, draws a sleeve across his eyes, and shares with

Tee a look perhaps typical of their singular friendship—a look of delight, untempered, ending with a sort of giggle.

We began to file out. Most of us did, anyway. The Fruit Machine turned. Baroque flute resumed playing. With those who were slated to perform the encore, I hid behind emptying risers, stage right. It was now the Final Interlude.

Miss Leith joined us. Did her hand brush my shoulder? I seem to recall it, and also her voice from somewhere behind me, her whispered head count. But I took no real notice. In that space, an alchemist's twilight held. Grown-ups clapped in silhouette, still standing, and the sound came down like a falls. Held flute notes appeared to take form on the backdrop—in mango, violet, pine green. I stood still. There was scent, I recall: something sweet, like candied apple. It was there and gone. I must have turned my head. I must have seen the light toss of her skirt, her vanishing leg. What I remember: the backstage curtain, its rich and ribbony folds, and how gently it swayed to conceal the breach—in the way of calm water, night water, moving inside itself. I reached. With the side of my cheek I pressed through.

Backstage, most of the lights were on. It took my eyes a few moments to adjust. As I recall, a wooden stepladder had been placed near the center of the floor, and something lay on its uppermost step, a branch, a long-stemmed flower. The school phonograph must have been here as well, with the 78 rpm flute recording wobbling beneath the tone arm, but this I can't place. There was only the ladder, the music, and a feeling—that all three of my teachers were here, Miss Leith, Mr.

Manfred and Tee, and that I should not be. Grazed by a draft, however, I drew forward. I could tell where the draft had come from: around a corner, a narrow hallway, a place at a growing distance from the source of the music, the sources of light . . .

What I saw: a doorway, the door itself halfway open. An iron grill landing beyond. An exit sign, cardboard, nailed to the plaster above. And I saw my teacher. Miss Leith stood leaning at the end of the hall, peering through the half-open door. Her breast did not rise. It was as if all rhythm of life in her had been stilled—so that chin and calf might be held just so. Air played at the hem of her skirt. That movement, though brief and not technically hers, triggered a sense of misgiving, which, as in dreams, seemed to intensify the things that were here in my view. The cardboard exit sign. The landing. All changed without changing. I looked at my teacher's frame, which did not move; and yet, as in dreams, I was afraid that it would, and afraid of what I would then see, and afraid that the whole stilled world had been awaiting just this—the advice of my fear.

And in fact she did turn. Face streaking, legs heaving: it was as if she'd exploded, as if the parts of her body were leaving in separate flight, and I could not move. I was helpless even to avert my face. She came with her mouth spread wide on a spooling sound that might have been *Ah*, though I don't recall hearing, and now Mr. Manfred was there in pursuit—somehow vaudevillian, though not in a comical way.

Then both were gone.

Judy Hente has had little to say as to the significance

of what happened backstage that night. Perhaps she's jealous. I'm the sole custodian of this; perhaps she wishes to deny the memory credence by withholding conjecture. I myself, in any event, have a theory, and will not pretend otherwise. Though it's possible, of course, that Miss Leith was set off by a discovery that would now seem trivial (had Tee and Reed Manfred uncorked champagne? Were they drinking in celebration?), I personally believe that what happened was this: she saw him, Tee, in those clothes of his, the tan suit with the brown embroidery; she saw him up-close, but with the unusual advantage of not being seen herself; saw him cleanly, that is—in the suit, in the crisp tan hat—whereupon she made the connection: all at once, she understood: he was not who he said, this man with whom she'd flirted conservatively, to whom she'd begun so carefully to entrust her unused heart. Now she knew who he was, this man. She knew his true name, its five syllables. She'd heard them, irrelevant before, but dividing him now from the town and its life—from her.

She knew who he was. She knew he could never be hers. When she fled that backstage hallway, it was in utter devastation.

I never saw Gable Roy Henry again. Did he leave before the lights came up for the encore? Did he walk the lonely service road, the neck of a bottle of alcohol loose in his picking hand? Or did he stay? Was he there when Mr. Manfred raised his arms like a bird and we twelve joined hands? I'd like to think so. He gave so much of himself; it would be a pity for him to have missed that final moment, which is still remembered by some: Reed Manfred catching the eyes of his singers, his baton a still point in the air, and drawing breath, and something beginning then, moving from hand to hand and opening into the senseless lyrics. Gable Roy Henry, as much as Reed Manfred, had made this moment possible. So it would be a pity if he didn't see us. It would be a pity if he wasn't there in wings surveying the standing room-only crowd, where, as I'd learn in the aftermath, even men like my father and Eldon Leith were visibly affected.

Is That You, John Wayne?

The day kept changing. The sky would close in virtual dusk and thunder from the other side of the river would rumble the sodden hill. Then something would open. For a while the birds would sing their song to the shining grasses.

"Who are you going to believe?" she said. "Me or your own eyes?"

He turned from the window. He said, "*Duck Soup*?"

"Only bad witches are ugly."

"Too easy," he said to her. "*Wizard of Oz*."

She lay on the wrinkled futon couch and worked a gathered lock of her hair into a very tight braid. She wore underwear and her breasts spread out within her tank top, which was charcoal gray.

"We didn't need dialogue," she said.

"We had faces," he responded. "*Sunset Boulevard*."

"You are somewhat good at this, aren't you?"

"Somewhat?"

He was joking but his heart wasn't in it. Through the screens, the light was in sudden decline, as if the fires of the sun had been doused. The live oak tree was a hex in the gloom and the bushes on the hillside were graves. He wondered why he felt like he'd known her so long. He wondered what they were doing for dinner. He wondered when he'd feel like he thought he would feel at his age, which tomorrow was thirty.

She lifted and kicked her shining legs in order to roll upright.

"You know, maybe I was wrong and luck is like love," she said.

He smiled. "Yeah."

"You know it."

"Do the next part."

"You already know it."

"Please?"

"Maybe I was wrong and luck is like love. You have to go all the way to find it."

"*Out of the Past.*"

She looked through the screen toward the picnic table which bore an assortment of last night's bottles glinting in a flourish of light. He watched her in profile. She seemed to have left herself there.

"Another?" he said too softly, almost at a whisper— he wasn't sure why.

She looked his way. It took her a few seconds to see.

"You give me your guess," she said to him. "I'll tell you if you've got the right one."

In response he laughed in an easy way, as if he understood. Then he did—understand. He knuckled the rough of his jaw. Her eyes were the light on his skin.

THE BOMB

He fashions the Bomb on a Tuesday in March. He sees it arise in sliding code on the screen of his office computer in the way that one sees the emerging motif of a simple doodle in pencil lead. He is talking on the phone—"I got you," he is saying. "Will do"—the first time the program runs.

A co-worker happens to see it, the Bomb, and stops at the entrance to his cube, and seems to debate asking, then asks in a way that he likes—with real interest and something like fear. And he tells her, "Oh, that," and devotes the next hour to the making of an icon—square, unbordered, deep gray, containing an uncentered 'x'— and an install component.

And the program is still nothing at all, so small that it can travel by email.

"In case you might want one," he writes to the co-worker, and reads it, and eventually clicks 'SEND.'

Five days later he cuts through a cubicle aisle on the other end of the 9th Floor. The Bomb leaves nothing of itself on the screen but a ghosted clone of the system clock, stalled at the exact moment the Bomb is erased, and he is astonished to see this faint double on the screen of a stranger, a middle-aged man whose bald head appears dented in the low yellow light.

And now he starts looking. He wanders the cubicle aisles. He keeps count.

Four. Seven. Twelve.

And maybe because the Bomb is now clearly beyond him, its effect on him grows. On days when the simple randomizer produces the oblong block on his screen, black and void—like an error, a failure of some kind—he stops. He forgets what he's doing. And if he's watching, even peripherally, when the numbers which finally appear in the block complete their five-minute run, he lets his eyes close, or pulls to the dark of his mind, and bestows himself gently, as if he were his own child, to the feeling that comes to him next.

Torrent of glass. Whirling blizzard of fire.

"Hey, thanks!" he hears one day from the woman to whom he first emailed the Bomb. "That's so cool!"

Through blinking eyes he searches her face. He says, "Great." He says, "Yeah."

In May, he emails his cousin, a first-year associate at a law firm in Denver. Since the Bomb is not really a bomb, even in loose terms—since the zeros at the end of its count yield nothing more spectacular than their own disappearance from the screen—he writes of the program, which he has attached, as if it's no more than a trifle. "I did this up on a slow afternoon," he writes. "A few people here like it."

His cousin responds immediately. "Already have it. You designed it, you mean?"

As he reads he begins sweating.

Search engines don't produce anything at first—the

Bomb is not inscribed with its name. Then he finds forums with topics devoted to the Bomb, blogs with the download provided.

In June the Bomb is discussed, albeit dismissively, on a cable news program. He begins to feel lost. He feels like more of him is erased than was ever there.

When his cousin, the lawyer, gets back to him, arguing that copyright hasn't been ceded, he moves quickly. In two days, he secures a domain—desktopbomb.com—designs a website, and adds to the package of the Bomb itself a set of display options, a new logo, a history menu, and a feature that causes the four zeros in the count box to shake before the Bomb disappears.

On July 1st he goes live. Few visitors arrive in the first seven days, and even fewer the next. He will not be discouraged. He works hard to promote the new Bomb, never pausing when it comes to his own screen. He is animated by a chance. Of major sponsorship. Ascension. The picture is inexact, but he feels it. Open rise.

NOTE TO DICKWAD EX-STEPDAD

It was me stole your wallet in Red Owl that time and squirted in Gulden's brown mustard. Not stole—found. On black-and-white checkerboard floor in the wake of your cart, Moron Man. Because you were drunk. Or had been when you woke us all up coming in the night before. Making noise. Breaking shit. Tell me something, Mayonnaise Brain: why did she always make pancakes for you after a night like that? Why were the sounds of fork on plate so quiet, so peaceful almost?

VIRGINITY

My girlfriend serves dinner in a retirement home and gets me a job washing dishes. She has to wear a white dress, heavy and unfashionable but all right with her body inside it. I can wear whatever, the clothes that I've gone to school in. It doesn't matter. I won't be seen.

"I used to come here a few years ago," I tell her.

We're out in the alley. She leans to my hands for a light.

"They let me out of fourth and fifth periods on Wednesdays if I would come read to this old lady."

My girlfriend stares at me. "Is she still here?"

I remember the name on the plaque on the door, Mrs. Sierra Cook. But I can't remember which floor. Five, maybe? I think it was five.

My girlfriend's dress is a white glow in the hallway as we creep along, reading names.

I say, "Maybe four."

Mrs. Sierra Cook, we learn, isn't living on the fourth floor either.

Later, we peer through the kitchen-door glass at the residents, who are taking their seats. They start to look faded, like plants in closets. Dried. Some are speaking, but we can't hear.

That night in the loft above her mother's garage, my girlfriend asks if I want to. The words are a surprise.

As we take position, she's looking at me. She's looking up carefully into my eyes, as if she is going to see the exact color of the change in me as it happens.

IN LIEU OF MY FINAL PAPER

Prodigious thanks, first of all, Professor Saloman, for considering what I wrote in my March 12th email and granting me an Incomplete. You yourself could not hope for such clemency if you tried emailing us with excuses like mine and saying you could not give us grades. I am very aware of this. Awareness in general is definitely on the rise in my case—even as I deal with the confusion of my parents' divorce and my Mother's collapse—and for this I place a heaping portion of credit squarely where it belongs, Professor. On your doorstep.

As promised, I have relinquished plans for Spring Break '03 and charged my amigo, Trip, with enjoying the careless spill of flesh in Daytona for the both of us. I have stayed on in Farlisburg, picking up shifts at the franchise restaurant where I wait tables and writing this Paper, which has veered quite a bit from the mold of the Paper that you assigned but which, I am hoping, will exhibit many of the qualities you believe in. I have, for example, "(experimented) with form," as you will see, and tried to "delve beyond surfaces, making discoveries as (I) go" (Your Assignment, Page 1).

But before the Critical Analysis gets going, let me say that your work in livening up a Core Requirement like English 1 has not gone unnoticed. Just last week I heard someone reciting the names of Professors from the Spring Course Bulletin, and someone else saying, when the first student had come to your name, "Saloman is the man you want." Modesty will keep you from acquiring a big head when you read this, knowing you. Of course I don't—know you. If ever I seemed to presume too far in that direction, I am sorry, really. The enduring regret: that my manifold character flaws may have done something to block the emergence of warm feeling between the two of us. Admiring you as I do, I would naturally prosper in the glow of your regard. It is my hope that once you have seen this Paper and considered what I have achieved you will be moved to think of me differently and allow such prospering.

"Friday, March 21, '03" (or "Introduction")

In today's society, Professor, the scourge of alcoholism is more and more plentiful. According to the National Institute of Drug Abuse, more than a quarter of a million Americans are currently in treatment for the insidious affliction (http://www.nida.nih.gov/Infofacts.html). Not counted in such figures are the dipsomaniacs who have not yet brought themselves to acknowledge their evident problem, or people like my Mother, whose abuse of alcohol is very prodigious on select occasions, like when she is collapsing, like she is right now.

"Tell that nice young steroidal fellow behind the bar

to bring along another drink when he can," she said recently, in a voice quite voluble.

This happened at the restaurant a couple of nights ago, on Friday (see heading above). I had just run my tabs through the register and clocked out. Next to my Mother's purse on the bar my black waiter's apron lay folded; open before me but not yet touched was a yellow legal pad. As of then, I had not yet hit upon a good Topic for this Paper, and thus was taking the advice you gave and thinking about undertaking a useful Prewriting Exercise.

I said to my Mother, "I've got a Paper to write, Ma."

"So you can't get me another drink?"

"So I can't supervise you."

"What does that mean? When in your entire miserable little life have I ever asked you to supervise me?"

"*Hey*," I said, because the barkeep, R.T., had come over.

"Miserable little skunk," said my Mother.

"She'll have another. And could I have—how about one of those seasonal ales?"

"Deluded little porcupine."

My Mother pressed a knuckle up into her nostril in the silence that followed. She wiped the corner of an eye. Feeling unable to endure R.T.'s service, which I took to be overly attentive, I looked toward the four big TVs mounted on drop bars. The war was on a couple of them—black video of Tomahawk missiles hitting Saddam's palace on the Tigris River—and March Madness on the others. North Carolina-Wilmington vs.

Maryland. A pretty good game.

"For this Paper, we're supposed to analyze something," I eventually said to my Mother. I explained about "(taking) a step back" from our world and seeing some part of it in a totally new way, without assumptions (Your Assignment, Page 2). I went on to discuss the great value of the process. Then I asked if she had any ideas.

My Mother didn't answer; she was giving me the silent treatment. I elected to remain optimistic, though, and ignore this.

"I mean, I look around, but what is there to question the assumptions of?" I said. To illustrate my meaning, I looked away from my Mother, swinging my attention to and fro. An NC-Wilmington guy, I saw, was bouncing the ball at the free-throw line; above the benighted Tigris River the same bright fires rose.

I then had an idea. "You think I could write about this place?" I asked. "How people might assume they're getting a 'unique dining experience,' like the commercials say, but if we take a step back—is the dining experience actually truly *unique*—I mean, if we really consider the definition of that word?"

I was deep in thought, Professor. For that reason, I had failed to take note of the fact that my Mother was silently getting worked up about something as she sucked on her drink.

"Do you believe someone's watching over us, John? I do. And that someone is laughing at me. Guffawing. Just pouring the laughter down over my head. Great buckets of laughter."

"The question is if I believe that? No."

My Mother looked at me. "You believe something different."

"I guess."

"Like what?"

"I don't know."

"For example."

"You know I'm not good under pressure," I said.

"Tell me this: when's the last time you washed your hair?"

Unwelcome scrutiny of my person and clothes arrived on the heels of the above comment. We can skip the details. I will say that my eventual apology—for not being, as I put it, 'more image-obsessed'—was sullen in a justified way.

"Are you even wearing underwear?" my Mother inquired of me in the next moment.

I said, "What?"

My shirt had come out of my pants on one side, and she made a quick grab for my belt loop—a maneuver I deftly but gently repelled.

"So I guess you're feeling a little better," I said.

"You're not. You're not wearing any underwear."

"Because usually—when you get really critical of people?—you're on an upswing. So that's good. You're on an upswing. See?"

"We grown-ups do laundry so we have clean clothes," said my Mother.

I sighed. "It's Finals Week."

Just then, a deep, collective "Oh" arose from the men at the bar. I waited for the replay: Maryland had won the game on a last-second, off-balance three. It was truly

momentous. I encouraged my Mother to watch, fearing
that she was going to miss out.

"Saturday, March 22, '03" (or "Body")

Knowing you, you will have made definite note of my
fun and creative decision to provide no Thesis in my
Introduction. You will be wondering, *What's up?*

Also you may be wondering why I have so far
withheld the name of the franchise restaurant where I am
employed.

Let us attend to such mysteries.

You see, Professor Saloman, if I had told you the
name of the restaurant, you might have been struck by a
certain coincidence of personal nature and thus have lost
track of the delicate flow of what I was saying at the time,
which would not have been good, considering my
mission as Writer is keeping you "fully (engaged)" (Your
Assignment, Page 2).

What I mean: after my Mother had bid me goodbye,
Friday night, I toured the restaurant floor, wondering if I
could do this Paper on the supposed uniqueness of our
dining experience. The prospect of such a Writing
Project did not really fire me up, yet I toured in good
faith. I was trying to "take a step back" from the familiar
booths and tables, to form new impressions—Critical
impressions, I hoped. I wondered if you might be
interested in our choice of music, adult contemporary. I
wondered if you would make anything of the fact that
every table bore, in a see-through plastic frame, a picture
of our currently featured app, the South O' the Border

Egg Rolls. And while I was wondering some of this, what did I see?

You in the flesh!

As it happened, I did not really see you so much as glimpse you, instinct leading me to remain unseen myself. But what I saw I saw clearly. A constellation of glittering details slowly rose through the sky of my mind, Professor. And the following day, after lunch rush was through, I embarked upon writing them down.

Cushioned booth, four-top
Set for two

Professor Saloman
Student (Lindsey? Lynnette?)

To have got something down on paper at last produced within me a good feeling. In order to experience it fully I set down my pad and relaxed in the backed stool. On TV was the expected fare: two second-round games, Missouri-Marquette and Arizona-Gonzaga, and the war, now in daylight. A correspondent was having the anchorman think of the capabilities of the posse of tanks that was being shown as it sped toward Baghdad.

I mention this because my Father, when he appeared at the bar, became interested and did not say hello.

"Hello," I said finally.

"John," said my Father.

"Dad."

"Son."

"Now that we've got that covered," I laughed, "what

are you doing here?"

My Father closed his eyes. "I deserve that."

"I wasn't being serious."

"No, I deserve it."

"Maybe I was a *little* annoyed because of how you sat down without saying hello . . ."

"No, no. I deserve it. I do."

A little background: my Father is dating someone. She is young and according to my Mother clinically obese. She works in a flower shop. I had not seen him for a period of maybe two weeks when he seated himself at the bar.

Further background, quite relevant if you bear with me, Professor: my Mother has often voiced the idea that men are either Drips or Pigs, and that ladies are well-advised to look for one who splits the difference (see Figure below).

In my Father she thought she had found such a man but turned out not to be right. Having wearied of men toward the Pig side, she overcorrected, she used to say. As refreshing as a man who is un-Piggish may be, a woman must always take care to make sure he is not a covert Drip.

I used to hope that my Father would think she was just being funny when she talked this way. She always looked like she was being funny. And he looked like he might have thought so. He would twist up his lips in an amused scowl.

Maybe she was trying to anger him, Professor—to create a good set of conditions for behavior more Piglike. In my opinion, however, she did not really think that my Father could ever be a Pig, and he did not think so himself, which probably factors in to how glad he now is to take the blame in the matter of the flower-shop girl.

He was hoping to discuss it at the bar, in fact, but I had to get back to this Paper.

"Question for you," I said to him. "You see two people in a place like this, eating dinner. A man and a woman. How much can you tell about them, just on sight? What do you know—" and I apologize for quoting you without citation, Professor— "just from the 'visual information'?"

"A man and woman," my Father repeated.

"Right."

"Involved?"

"No assumptions," I said. "We know nothing. What can be told?"

"Well, I would think you could tell if they were involved or not. Obviously there's some kind of relationship between them. Over time you'd be able to guess which kind and say something about the tenor of that relationship as well."

"This is good," I said, grabbing my legal pad. "The *tenor of the relationship.*"

"*T. E. N. O. R.*"

"So what would you look at?"

"Well, how are they sitting?" my Father said after a

moment. "Where do their eyes go? How are they dressed?"

"Yes."

"What kinds of expressions do we see on their faces? Are they drinking? What are they eating?"

"Yes."

"This is about Sapphire and me, isn't it?"

"No."

My Father put a hand on my forearm.

You appeared comfortable, Professor Saloman. You sat back, with one arm extended atop the plump cushion that accepted your weight. You were speaking. Two uneaten potato skins lay within reach of your softly gesticulating hand, as did a squat brown bottle of beer, likely a pricey domestic. You had rolled up your sleeves—the sleeves of your white button shirt—as often you will in class, and your arm hair showed, blond-brown, along with the gold bracelet of your watch. From my vantage point I could not see quite as much of your companion—Lindsey or Lynnette, I believe ('L,' I propose she be called). She leaned into the table, bracing herself on her arms, which were crossed, and holding her shoulders and back quite straight considering the angle. Her hair—brown hair—she had gathered and pinned up in back. Bright tendrils hung floatingly down.

Recalling one of your lectures on Critical Analysis, I asked, What if things had been different? What if Professor Saloman had been the one sitting forward in so crisp a way? What if L had been the one to recline and gesticulate? This strategy was useful, just as you claimed it would be. Revelations did not come flooding in, though. Your being a Professor, and L's being a student of yours, seemed to account for most of what I could conclude from my glimpse of your table.

I had come to a dead end, Professor. I was beginning to doubt myself, to wonder what I had been thinking when I had been thinking I might have a Topic.

Then I opened my backpack and glanced at a handout I had looked through just a few days earlier when preparing for my Final in Psych. And what I encountered, bathed in lemony-yellow highlighter, was indeed germane.

In today's society, Professor Saloman, laughter is prevalent. It is fairly low profile, however, not being frequently discussed or even considered. Enter Dr. Robert Provine. Believe it or not, this person has done a full study on the subject, asking, for example, what laughter might mean in the case of a man and a woman together. There are various answers in his works, but one thing he says which you might find intriguing is this: the "laughter of the female, not the male, is the critical positive index" when you are wondering how good a time both are having, the man and the woman together (Provine, 35).

Does the woman laugh? That is Provine's question.

And L did. In a minor way—and so softly, it seemed, that you yourself might not have heard—L laughed at what you said. She did not seem unserious, laughing, but she laughed, and for Provine this signaled a healthy connection—which only made sense, I was thinking, because why would a Professor and student be dining in the first place if that were not so?

Now I was energized. Around me the afternoon people were gathering to drink and watch hoops or the war, but I barely even noticed. "If Provine is right," I wrote, pinching the craw of the pen with escalating fervor, "L's laughter may also be speaking to us of their desire to get together again soon."

I could now see my path. I would "do all (I) could to answer those questions that (had arisen) in the course of (my) work" (Your Assignment, Page 1). I would "develop (my) thinking on the subject . . . via careful and pointed research" (ibid).

I tracked down my boss.

"Who's doing your prep work?" he said. "Are you on?"

"About that . . ."

"Oh no you don't."

"Seriously," I said to him.

"*Seriously*," he responded.

In time I was able to lead him to see that my getting kicked out of school once more was not in anyone's interest. I jogged out to my car. Waiting to pull into traffic, I called up my Mother and asked if my Father had left his binoculars when he moved out.

As I am sure you are aware, Professor Saloman, two paths rise from the gully that borders the north and east sides of your back yard. The larger and closer of the two, unfortunately, offers no view of your second-story windows. I was thus in a position of having to contest the thick brambles of the second path—the one "less traveled," as a Great Writer might have said (Frost, 24).

Thrills attended my climb and the establishment of my position, I will confess. I kept hearing narration, like I was on TV.

> *He arrives at the head of the path. Using the brush as camouflage, he lifts and adjusts the binoculars and performs swift reconnaissance.*

In time, though, my legs started falling asleep, and I had to admit to myself that I was not in fact seeing too much. Briefly I spied you in the kitchen, Professor. You reached for a wooden cutting board, I believe; you peeled and then sliced some fruit. Otherwise, nothing arose in the jiggly frame of my Father's binoculars to rupture the numbing stillness of your foursome of boxy back rooms.

I had a plenitude of time to consider such things as the calendar hanging in your kitchen. Did its skillfully rendered watercolor of a jalopy mean you were an enthusiast of old cars?

And to consider your guest room: if a single man keeps puzzles and toys on shelves, what is that to say? That a child visits him? A child from wherever he lived last year, before coming to Farlisburg?

Such questions led me, naturally enough, to muse on the one thing I knew of your past, and muse, too, on my careless mention of it in the hall after the first day of class. You see, I am a fool for coincidence, Professor. I never thought to question the urge to tell you that the old *alma mater*, in your case, and the illustrious institution I had recently transferred from were one and the same. How strange, I was thinking, that we found ourselves here, so far from the handsome, heavily endowed school just west of Philadelphia. What a small world.

Unfortunately you may not have taken my comments exactly as hoped, Professor. I wince to imagine what thoughts you may have had in those moments after I proffered my hand and shared with you what I did. Maybe you saw me as trying to seem superior to my fellow students, or to the work of the class itself. Maybe you saw me as trying to draw you to look upon Farlisburg, and all it encompassed, as a relative joke. Such a deleterious hypothesis (for me) might have found seeming support in my failure, thereafter, to show up regularly or turn in assignments on time.

I have already bent your ear too much with apologies and excuses, Professor. But know this: I cannot write a paragraph like the one I just wrote and feel good. I should have guessed I could not say 'Swarthmore' to you without our both having to think, on some level, how none of the other students in class could ever have gotten in there. I have to say I am frustrated: my whole East Coast experience, although done, continues to bite me in the butt. May I be shot point-blank through the head the next time I bring it up.

Where was I?

Your house. Your back yard. The second of your paths from the gully.

Being that it was Saturday night, my boss possessed reasonable expectations of us getting totally slammed. Thus I had to return. By 6:00 at the latest, he had said.

And so, at half-past or thereabout, I capped my Father's binocular lenses and somewhat incautiously rose to begin working the blood back into my legs. I say 'somewhat incautiously' because right at that moment—another coincidence, Professor Saloman!—your back door drifted in on its hinges and you came drifting out. Needless to say, I was sweating. Soon, though, I was able to make out in your mood some softness that worked in my favor. You had not come to survey your property. No. Your gaze traveled out past the line of the trees and into the downcoming blues and grays of the towering eastern sky. Arrested in waning fear, but arrested, I watched you open your breast, as it seemed, to the almost painful loveliness of the swiftly approaching night. I wondered if you were thinking about a child who visited your house sometimes, or a student who enjoyed your company and whose company you enjoyed. I could not know. Our obliquely shared moment, therefore, acquired a poignancy.

In today's society, Professor Saloman—this is according to my Mother—a lady is well-advised to be reading a book if she hopes to dine out by herself and not have everyone look at her. Since my Mother cannot read in public, though, she has to employ the ruse of an open paperback on her table. That night, it was *If on a Winter's Night a Traveler*, by Italo Calvino—a Great Writer who is not from this country.

"Is it any good?" I asked as I was taking her order.

"I wouldn't know," said my Mother. "But I love the title. Endless possibilities."

I nodded. "Blue Cheese, Ranch, Italian, French or Honey Mustard?"

"Oh, my."

"On your salad."

"I see."

"Honey Mustard," I said. Not hearing complaints, I wrote down and circled 'HM' on my pad and turned and made for the kitchen.

My boss had predicted correctly. We were slammed. In contrast to the night before, my Mother was not drinking, and was looking, as a result, more dignified but also less solid, less sure. I felt bad zipping past her two-top as I saw to the needs of larger parties. A few sightings of the folded lemon wedge beached on the tea-colored cubes of ice in her glass were enough for me to apprehend it as a Symbol, Professor Saloman, standing for all of my failings as Son, all of her disappointments as Mother.

"More iced tea!" I said to her finally, and poured.

As a rule, whenever I count on my Mother for some kind of zippy remark, she fails to provide one.

"I got a Topic for that Paper," I offered.

"Oh?"

"A good one, too, I think."

"Would you like me to ask you what it is?"

I giggled.

"What is it?"

I straightened my shoulders and looked her in the eye and without really knowing the reason came out with a lie that afterward fascinated me. "Love," is what I said to my Mother. "The Topic of my Paper is Love."

*

I got off at 10:30. With one of the kitchen guys I smoked a cigarette in the alley. With another waiter I had a beer. Then I went out and got in my car and drove east—heading home, I might have said, though my evident decision to detour through your quiet neighborhood came as no shock.

As you might recall, you had drawn the curtains in your living-room windows, Professor Saloman, but strong yellow light could be seen at the sides, as if leaking from careful incisions. I slowed down to gaze longer. I was not really planning to do as before—to park and approach through the gully—but the curtained light drew me. It seemed to address me, Professor—about things that are "taken for granted," and how these things can "emerge in sharp focus" from within their taken-for-grantedness, like a snake wriggling out of his dried-up skin (Your Assignment, Page 2; metaphor mine).

That is to say I was feeling very tuned in to something unknown as of yet. With alacrity I could thus read the meaning of the car beside yours in the driveway, the Nissan Sentra, with the solo sticker in back—"U.S. Out of My Uterus!"—and the student-parking decal in front.

"L," I said in a grave whisper.

I moved out past the edge of the gully, into the grass of your back yard. The blinds in the upstairs windows were down, but small fluctuations within the soft light had me thinking that you and your visitor were there, and that somebody might thus enter without being heard, provided the door was unlocked.

And it was—just as I guessed it would be when I

thought of you opening it earlier that day in order to look at the sky.

I could at this point dawdle, and describe the scent of cinnamon, or the vacuumed Oriental runner in the hall, or the shining secretary with the crystal penholder on top, all of which I liked, and which gave me a pleasant and unexpected appreciation of your homemaking skills.

I did not really dawdle at the time, though. At the time, I moved slowly, quietly and directly up your stairs.

You would not have a reason to remember this, Professor, but the door to your room was ajar. And so, the second I turned on your newel post, I could see a certain part of what I admit I had already recognized the sound of. I would not say this was my intention—to see you. Then again I could not say the opposite. In a way, I doubted the news of my ears; I did not yet believe what I believed. In that sense, seeing you was useful, I guess, but let me say plainly one thing in case it is not clear: I was quite unprepared.

You had assumed the posterior position, Professor. When you curled down over L's back I could see your face and your eyes were closed. I could not see L's face, but once when you raised yourself straight I believe I heard the pillow snap free of her teeth. How balanced you were, I was thinking. Not Drip—not at all. And not Pig. I watched for some time, until my experience in your hallway threatened to morph into something yet stranger. To phrase it in a manner appropriate, I hope, to the discourse we've got going here: I began to perceive the unwanted effect that watching you and L was having on me.

If you thought you heard someone descending your stairs, moving in a fast and flustered way, you were on target. It was I, Professor.

"Sunday, March 23, '03" (or "Conclusion")

When you were at Swarthmore, did Sharples run the dining halls? If so, did they offer Burrito Bar? No one admits to liking the food of Sharples, I am aware, but I did like Burrito Bar. Nowadays on occasion I will try and recreate it, using whatever has been prepped in the kitchen. Taco meat, onion, sliced jalapenos, tomato, salsa, cheese—all of this went in today. Since morning I had been lodged in the process of writing, tapping the laptop keys, and was hungry. I took the completed burrito to the bar on an oval salad plate, and as I did I had a thought both simple and profound: nobody knows why anyone else does all the small things that he does. Nobody watching me carry my lunch to the bar could even begin to unlock the meaning of a burrito for me, just as I could not begin to unlock, for example, the meaning of hair gel for the college-hoops fan to my left.

What's the deal with the laptop? this man might have wondered about me.

Wherefore the prodigious interest in Purdue basketball? I might have asked.

It is like we are all these huge encyclopedias of secrets, Professor Saloman. In reality, though, we do not so much ask questions—except maybe in cases like these, when we have a chance to write and become involved with Critical Thinking.

I am remembering your expressed distaste for conclusions that "tell us what you have told us," Professor. In homage to that particular comment, I will be going for concision and pointedness here.

As a Great Writer whom I recommend highly might say, you managed to perceive with "the eyes of (your) eyes" that the strictures dividing you and L were based on assumptions quite arbitrary (http://en.wikiquote.org/wiki/E._E._Cummings). In a similar way, I managed to squeeze through a hole in what I was taking for granted about you and L, and discover the truth. And in regard to that discovery—its awkwardness aside . . . how odd! How wild an occurrence, Professor! A moment beyond any one person's feeble power to concoct!

As I move toward closing, I sense a need to address the delicate issue of grading. You see, Professor Saloman, I need to pass this class to graduate. If you felt you could not review this Paper without bias, considering its subject matter (you), I would definitely understand and would just ask that you pass it along to a third party—Professor Grass, for instance, the new Chair of your Department. I have heard he is a very fair grader.

Practicality of an unpleasant sort leads me to advance the above scenario. I hope things will go differently. I hope you will end up being the one to read this with pen in hand. I hope you will compare it to others you received—those written by students who seemed to keep more to the assignment—and will find much to like. I know I have worked hard. Any comments you have for me would be greatly appreciated, Professor Saloman.

*

I will close by speaking of a break I took from the writing earlier today. Thinking about my good buddy Trip, I had turned from the war to Spring Break on one of the TVs. A big tug of war was apparently just getting started. The girls seemed to fall with some frequency, and when they did the sand would stick to those places not covered by their bikinis. I had a beer as I watched. As I was downing the foamy dregs of it, who should show up but my Father. He was worried about my Mother, he explained without preamble. He wondered if we could talk.

Maybe because I was then writing the part of this Paper about Robert Provine, I referred to Provine's question and said that my Mother would feel better if she could do more of the laughing in her relationship with God.

"Did you just say 'God'?" asked my Father.

"The other day she told me she thought He was laughing at her."

"Did she use that word?"

"'Laughing'?"

"No."

"What word?"

My Father seemed to be calculating something.

"'God'? She didn't say that exactly, no."

"You know, John," he said quite carefully. "We chose to do what seemed best at the time in giving you a secular upbringing. Occasionally, though, it occurs to me that you might on your own experience the inclination to 'seek', spiritually speaking. And I want you to know—"

"I'm not seeking," I said.

Not buying this, my Father nodded.

"Maybe I am seeking a little but not in the way that you mean," I said, whereupon I made a confession of the fact that I am coincidence-smitten.

To believe in coincidence, I explained, is to look for signs that the seeming dislinearity of our lives may be only illusion—that we are connected, in other words. To the past. And to each other. To believe in coincidence, I went on, is to know that meaningful patterns are there, waiting to be divined.

I said these things in an abstract way, more abstract than you might think. I said them with enthusiasm. I am not sure what my Father could get, but he looked pleased.

Swarthmore, of course, had been on his dollar.

"How's the Paper coming?" he said.

Considering the question, I nodded my head, and nodding, I felt like the Argus of yore, master of my environment. I saw everything, Professor: the round slices of hard-boiled egg on top of someone's Chef Salad, and the bouncing bikini girls, there on either side of the guy with the microphone, and the stars in the beer light, and the guys on the Purdue bench, and the jet on the carrier in the Gulf which was just lifting off at the angle of the phallus.

"Pretty good," I said to my Father then. "I think it's all coming together."

HOURLY

They gave me a job at Halloween Town. Strip mall with vacancies. Sad. I was a wizard, vaguely swinging my wand. "Everything change," I commanded.

INTERSTATE

My boy got sick in Montana so I pulled off the road.

Will we still see Grandma? he asked.

I put my hand on his forehead and said to be still.

I want to see Grandma, he said.

I had the wipers on delay, and they moved, sweeping mist from the glass.

You wait here? I asked when we'd rolled to a stop in the narrow porte-cochere.

He blinked, and his eyes looked right into mine, and he saw how bad and desperate I felt about this—his having to convalesce on the road, in a Super 8.

The cartoons were too fast, too antic.

When he closed his eyes, I was hoping for sleep.

Will you tell me a story?

I pushed the mute. I straightened the sheet across his shoulders.

One time, a few years before you were born, your Mom and I went camping.

Not about Mom, he said, and I looked at him.

All right.

Sweat had pasted a curl to his cheek. I opted to leave it alone.

*

I told him about Bearskin. Memory had beached the central details, but they were ornate in my mind.

A man, and he's wearing the skin of a bear—he has to. For years and years. A man, and he wanders. And strangers round their eyes and pull themselves into their bodies, or turn and flee, for he's dirty, he's ugly, he's wrong. And however bad the man may appear, he feels just so much worse.

Somehow he has money. Gold coins, useless things. A splatter on paving stones.

In truth he has faith—just that, nothing else: I will make it through.

That's not a good story.

How about you sleep for a while?

Why did he have to wear the skin?

I don't know. I can't remember.

When he woke, he looked better—less slack, less wan. On TV, something gentle played, and for this I was feeling grateful.

He drank some fresh water.

Then his Grandma called, and we put her on the speaker of my cell.

He said, Grandma, I'm sick.

She said, I know that, baby.

He said, I'm going to miss Halloween.

She spoke fiercely: about how we would do everything tomorrow, or whenever he arrived. The costumes, the carving of the pumpkin.

He listened. His face seemed vacantly pleased.

I went out for a smoke. But I left the room door open halfway, so he could see my shoulder.

Are there trick-or-treaters? he called.

I blew smoke. No.

Is there anything?

I called, Not really.

But it wasn't so. There was a moon, big and round, and telephone wires. An intersection, vehicles swishing. There was a sky. It was huge. Slow yellows and grays. I watched as if it was my duty.

PREMISES FOR AN ACTION PLAN

1.

Spencer Bray's picture was not among the pictures of faces the cops had me look at. The cops, as of a quarter past ten last night, knew nothing of Spencer Bray. Or they just weren't considering him as a person who might perpetrate a holdup of the Boone Street Gas 'n Go. Five-eleven, six foot, I said to the cops. Beefy. Black hair. All true information. Color? What? I said. Race, they said. White, I said. (True.)

Features? Eyes? Nose? Lips?

I don't know, I was scared, I was the one getting robbed. I did my best not to look up.

All true! The cops will not be able to say, Rory Jeffery, we know that you lied.

2.

Pumping gas outside as the money was taken: W. Voss, who was questioned too.

She may not have had a good angle. She was close but may not have been looking at us when Spencer Bray clapped his small firearm down, holding it to the counter like a mouse, and lifted his ski mask—which was mustard-colored, as I reported, and ribbed—to scratch at his face.

She may not have seen him, or recognized him as himself—the kid who had cheerfully terrorized us on the grounds of Wright Elementary.

Then again she might have. And if she did, she'd have given the cops his name.

She's that kind of person. She's never not paying attention in AP Economics. That's why she can be looked at.

3.

And if she did give the cops his name and offer the fact that she and Spencer and I had attended the same elementary, the cops might wish to talk further.

If that were the case, would they dial my cell? Do cops call people on their cell phones?

They'd use the home number.

And who would pick up?

4.

Therefore I can't be sure that by doing nothing I'm doing all that I can to prevent trouble with the cops, and trouble with M and D, who still don't know what happened last month—how our Buick was backed up into a Self-Service Island at the Boone Street Gas 'n Go on a super-cold night when I failed to push the button for rear defrost, and how, after that, I was able to forge a deal with the owner to work off the damage. (Knowledge of this would have to precede any sympathy I might get for being robbed.)

5.

Neither is there any clear action to take to *reduce* the risk of trouble with the cops and trouble with M and D.

6.

Therefore trouble of these two kinds should not be the primary concern.

7.

Do I know you? Spencer Bray asked. And I shook my head in the slightest possible way, not wanting to move. I know you. Wait.

And I wasn't looking at him but could feel his mirth coming in waves.

Wait. Hang on.

I peeked at his hand on the gun. I waited with all of

my might.

One scenario: recognition never comes to Spencer Bray. He forgets about thinking he knew me. Recognition never comes to W. Voss, either, so his name is not given to the cops, and the cops do not find him. Result: I'm home free.

Another scenario: recognition does come to Spencer Bray. He wakes in a bed in the house of one of those uncles or cousins he always stayed with, and sits up, and says, as the dust motes spin in the sunlight, *Rory Jeffery.* And he puts on his parka—red, as I reported. And puts his gun in its right-hand pocket. And finds me. And kills me. Shoots me right through my tetanus-shot scar, which is just where he once put the pocketknife blade on the grounds of Wright Elementary. The bullet glances the humerus, slips through the rib cage and explodes my heart.

Goodbye life. Goodbye W. Voss.

8.

Or this: recognition does come to Spencer Bray in a bed on the north side of town, but he stays calm, regarding me—correctly, I guess—as one of the kids he subdued for good a long time ago, on the grade-school playgrounds.

But recognition then comes to W. Voss, too (if it hasn't already), and she tells the cops, who she trusts from watching high-rated shows like *Law & Order.*

Everyone watches them. Can W be faulted?

In that one pair of jeans she has, in that tiny green shirt, as she paints her toenails, maybe, she watches the shows and trusts the cops and gives them the name, Spencer Bray. And they go to his house, or the house where his parents live. As I've indicated, though, he's never there!

So the cops don't get him. But he learns, through the family grapevine, that the cops are after him now, and he blinks his eyes, and he gets the red parka, the gun. And kills me.

That flat pink color, the toenails would be. Bubble gum. She applies it innocently, without asking what others might think about it.

Because she likes it. She likes that color.

9.

Or how about this: he awakes in that bed on the north side of town and says to himself, *Whitney Voss.* Those syllables slide into place as he remembers the girl he saw standing by Pump #3 as he left with the money I gave him.

He gets the red parka. The gun.

10.

I scrape the Buick's tire sides into the curb and sprint to her doorway.

Rory.

Whitney.

Listen.

But I'm out of breath.

And she waits without feeling infringed upon by this visit from this guy who's not much more than an acquaintance. The day may seem uneventful enough, but she's sensitive. Right away she's able to see we've been joined by the weather of crisis.

Or I take the left into W's cul-de-sac, passing Spencer on the sidewalk, in his parka, on foot.

Rory.

Whitney.

I close my hand around hers. There is no time to explain.

11.

RE: delayed recognition, though: how likely?

I recognized Spencer Bray. That's firm.

Spencer Bray didn't recognize me.

W. Voss did or didn't recognize him. But if she did, wouldn't the cops have called here already—if just to have me look at more pictures?

The day is quiet. In the yard, snow is melting. I'm looking at sopping brown leaves.

Rory? M calls.

Yes.

Rory?

Yes.

Would you take out the trash?

*

12.

What's likely: W. Voss, at Pump #3, didn't recognize Spencer Bray. It was darker out there, after all.

What's likely: Spencer Bray will forget about us—me and W. Voss. By the time the cops start looking for him—if they do—he won't even remember our faces.

Will the cops catch him?

They could. It's possible.

He could buy everyone tokens at the Southroads Arcade, say it's on the Boone Street Gas 'n Go. He might do that.

We'd be called to testify, me and W. Voss. And then he'd remember. *Rory Jeffery*, he'd think to himself. *Rory Jeffery. Whitney Voss.*

And how long could they keep him in custody? He's only sixteen years old.

Concerns of this kind—are they not serious? Do they not compel me to quit typing, right now? To stand from this lightweight swivel chair? Cross the floor of the walk-in basement?

They do.

Cross the floor. Get my cell phone. Flip up the screen. Press in W's number. Touch the cold glass of the doors as I wait. Examine the tree limbs, the power lines, the tiny sparkling crusts of snow out there by the chain-link fence.

ACKNOWLEDGEMENTS

"Starts" appeared in *Necessary Fiction*; "The Fake I.D." and "Is That You, John Wayne?" in *New Ohio Review*; "Demons" in *New Orleans Review*; "Say My Name" in *Everyday Genius*; "Advent Santa" in *The Kenyon Review* (KR Online); "Sofa" in *Quick Fiction*; "About Me and My Cousin" in *matchbook*; "At the Beach Hotel" in *5x5*; "The Goth of SecurityOne Field" in *Carolina Quarterly*; "Desultory" in *Redivider*; "The Fifty" in *New York Tyrant*; "Acquired from Ex-Girlfriends" in *Hobart*; "Hourly" in *Matter Press:* JOURNAL OF COMPRESSED CREATIVE ARTS; "Kiss of the Underachiever" in *The Literarian:* JOURNAL OF THE CENTER FOR FICTION; "I Knew Gable Roy Henry" in *Flyway*; "The Bomb" in *No Colony*; "Note to Dickwad Ex-Stepdad" in *Ping Pong:* JOURNAL OF THE HENRY MILLER LIBRARY; "Virginity" in *Unsaid*; "In Lieu of My Final Paper" in *Avery Anthology*; "Interstate" in *Mississippi Review*; and "Premises for an Action Plan" in *American Short Fiction*.

I need to thank everybody at those journals and these people in particular: Steve Himmer, Kathy Fish, Jill Allyn Rosser, Christopher Chambers, David Lynn, Jennifer Pieroni, Adam Pieroni, Brian Mihok, Edward Mullany, Brooks Sterritt, Giancarlo DiTrapano, Luke Goebel, Jensen Beach, Aaron Burch, Randall Brown, Dawn Raffel, Sam Pritchard, Blake Butler, Ken Baumann,

Jessica Breheny, David McLendon, Stephanie Fiorelli, Kim Chinquee and Stacey Swann.

For their particular support I need to thank some others: Arnold and Lynne Garson, David Scott, Deb Schmidt, Betsy Scott, Brian Thorniley, Laurie and Tom Bulka, Meg and Jason Hieronymus, Caitlin Horrocks and Kevin Wilson.

I can't list through all the readers, writers, friends and family whose enthusiasm has been so important to me, but I want them to know that I'm grateful.

Three names for last: Rebecca R. Scott, Chris Garson and Erin McKnight.

©Chris Garson

Scott Garson was born in Nebraska and grew up in Iowa. A graduate of Carleton College and George Mason University, he has received awards for his work from Playboy, the Mary Roberts Rinehart Foundation, and Dzanc Books. He lives with his wife and two children in central Missouri.

CPSIA information can be obtained at www.ICGtesting.com
Printed in the USA
BVOW071250060613

322631BV00002B/4/P